MATCH FOR THE COWBOY

HANNAH JO ABBOTT

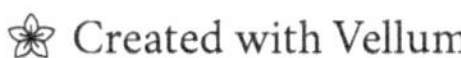

To our church family,
who loves us and supports us.
We're so thankful to have a community of believers like you to
do life with.

"I can do it," Colton Macklin said. He set his jaw and crossed his arms.

His brother, Lawson, smiled at him. "Thanks, little brother, but I think Garrett and I can handle it."

Colton ripped his cowboy hat off his head. "You just said we all need to step up. I can take over the cattle for a month. You're right, Sawyer doesn't need to worry about anything when the baby comes. You already have other responsibilities. If we hire some extra hands for the season, I can be in charge."

Hawk clapped a hand on the youngest brother's shoulder. "Thanks, Colt. We all know you're a hard worker. But overseeing the cattle business is a big job. Better let Lawson do it this time."

Colton turned and left the room without another word. Stomping out of the house, he let the front door slam as he stepped off the porch and mounted his horse. He ground his teeth as he gave the horse a nudge and set out for his own piece of the property.

"They never see me as anything but the baby. Just because I'm younger doesn't mean I can't handle the job."

When he reached the spot he wanted, he jumped down and let the horse graze. At least here he could be alone. This was his property. Each of his six brothers had their own spot on the family ranch, and this was his. Maybe it was time he started thinking about building a house and moving out of the one he'd grown up in. That would show them all. Only Sawyer and Jenson had built on their land so far. Colton knew they thought he would be last, since he was the youngest, but he could prove them wrong.

Colton heard hooves pounding the ground behind him and turned.

"Hey, you ran off before we could finish talking," Hawk said as he dismounted.

Colton turned to stare in the opposite direction. "I was done talking. And no one listens to me anyway."

"Yeah we do. It's just a big job, and Lawson's been working with Sawyer longer than you."

"I've been working on this ranch since I could walk."

"We all have," Hawk said. He laughed. "But you're right. I remember when you were two, walking around with a hammer and measuring tape. You never played with toys. You would get up and say 'Gotta go to work.' We all thought it was so cute."

"It's not cute anymore. I'm not a little kid. I'm a grown man, and I work as hard as anybody."

"Like I said, you left before we finished talking. I was going to say you could take over my job. I'll help Lawson and Garrett with running things, and you can handle the auctions."

Colton scowled. "Why? I don't know anything about

auctions. I work here with the cattle. I don't need your pity job. Everybody has their own responsibility around here, but I'm like a hired hand who's told where and when to work."

"Come on, man. It's not like that."

"It is too. You try being in my shoes for a day. But forget it. I'll keep working. One day y'all are gonna need me, and by then I just might have found my own job."

"Don't say that, bro. You know we want you here."

"Do I know that? Because you all seem to think you could handle it without me. I'd like to see what would happen if I wasn't here. Maybe I'm not in charge, but I do a lot of the work around here that nobody notices."

Hawk lifted his hat to wipe his brow with his arm before returning the hat. "I told you, we know you work hard. No one gets a medal around here. We all work hard. I'm sorry if you don't feel appreciated, but we all just do what we need to do. And right now we need to give Sawyer and Jenson a break. Lawson needs to be the one to step up this time. Your time will come."

"Sure it will." Colton turned and walked away. He waited as he heard Hawk let out a heavy sigh and go for his horse. When Hawk was gone, Colton turned back and went to his own horse. He stroked the animal's neck as he talked to himself. "They have no idea what I do around here. Everyone takes me for granted because I'm always here and do what needs to be done. They don't even see it."

Many times Colton had thought about leaving Whispering Oaks Ranch. Maybe somewhere else he would be more appreciated, or at least be treated like a man, instead of the baby of the family. Each of the brothers had their own thing. Sawyer was in charge, Jenson handled the horses, even Hawk and Lawson had responsibilities. But the youngest brother was left to follow orders and do grunt work. Maybe it was time to think about what his own thing would be.

As his mind ran over possibilities, Colton mounted his horse and nudged him into a gallop. He didn't know where he wanted to go, but it was time to get a move on.

***

GRACE ROGERS HAD CHECKED THE REARVIEW MIRROR A hundred times since she'd pulled out of the driveway before dawn that morning. Now Louisiana had disappeared from view, and the wide planes of Texas sprawled in front of her. She kept her speed reasonable on the interstate, despite the fact that she wanted to put distance behind her as quickly as possible.

She'd tried to tell her family that she needed to get out of the relationship with Blaine. They only assured her that everything was fine and she was being silly. Her mother was expecting an engagement ring on Grace's finger any day now. But Grace didn't have to wonder. Blaine had told her exactly when and where they would get engaged and married and where they would live. Just like he'd told her how he wanted her to wear her hair and clothes and that she could leave her job and take care of the house for them.

Grace wasn't going to sit around and wait for the future he was planning. She'd tried to break up with him more than once, but he wouldn't have it. This was her only way out.

The only problem was, she didn't know where she was going. She had an envelope of cash she'd taken from her bank account yesterday. Only last week Blaine had suggested they combine their accounts, and Grace was sure she was about to lose all chance of escape. But that money wouldn't last her long. She would need to find a place to stay and a way to earn money. How would she find a job without references? She couldn't list her former employer on an application. If they called her father's company, Blaine would find out where she was.

"God," Grace whispered, "please help me."

At that moment, she heard a strange sound, and her car started to rumble.

Her eyes grew wide, and she gripped the steering wheel until her knuckles were white. "Really?" she cried out. "That doesn't seem to be helping."

She looked up and saw the sign on the interstate for the exit. "Shelby Springs, six miles." Glancing around, she saw nothing in sight. No gas station off the interstate, no town. Shelby Springs seemed her only hope. If only she could make it that far.

Grace took the exit and prayed she could make it, but a few miles later, she knew she was in trouble. Smoke rose from the hood of the car. Shaking, Grace pulled off on the side of the road and cut the engine. She put her face in her hands and let the tears fall. So far she'd held it together. There was no time for tears. There still wasn't, but what else was she going to do?

"God, I asked for help, not to be stranded in the middle of nowhere. I can't even call for help." Her cell phone was tucked away in a drawer in her closet. She was sure Blaine would find a way to trace it. She had planned to pick up a new one when she got wherever she was going. Now it was too late.

Once she had cried it out, she wiped her tears and drummed her fingers on the steering wheel. It was probably time to get out and walk. She took a deep breath and reached for the ponytail holder on her wrist to tie up her long, dark hair. She would look like a hot mess before she walked far enough to get help, but what did it matter.

The sound of wheels on gravel alerted her, and she turned to see a pickup truck pull up behind her. She immediately felt relief and then fear. There was no way to know if the person was friend or foe. Grace stared into the mirror and watched as a man climbed from the cab of the truck and moved toward her. He wore jeans and a work shirt, and a cowboy hat sat atop his head. She definitely wasn't in Louisiana anymore. She watched as he glanced at the back of her car and took in the license plate.

He tipped his hat back and leaned down to her window. "Is everything all right, ma'am?"

Ma'am? When was the last time she'd been called that? "No, actually. My car started smoking, and I pulled off. I wasn't sure what to do."

He flashed a smile. "I'd be happy to take a look."

"Oh no, I don't want to put you out. But I don't have a phone. Could you call a tow truck to get me to the nearest garage?"

The man straightened and put his hands on his hips. "Sure, I can do that. But it's a hot day to sit out here waiting on a tow truck. That could take quite a while. I'd be happy to give you a lift somewhere so you don't melt."

Grace's heart slammed against her chest, and her

throat closed up. What might happen to her if she got in a car with a strange man in the middle of nowhere? "No, thank you," she managed to squeak out. "I'll just wait."

"You must be Grace."

She snapped her head to look at him, and she gripped the steering wheel as if her life depended on it. If she thought it would help, she would have turned the key. If only she could speed away as fast as possible. Had Blaine already sent someone after her?

He bent back down and put his hands on the window. "Sorry, I didn't mean to scare you. News travels fast in Shelby Springs. It's a pretty small place, you know. Pastor Judson told me you were coming."

"Oh, he did?" Grace said, confusion still on her face. Who in the world was Pastor Judson, and how did he know she was coming? She hadn't known she was coming.

"I'm sure you don't want to be late on your first day of work. I can give you a ride to the church. We can worry about the car later."

Her mind swam with ideas and worry. Should she go with this man? He seemed to believe she was supposed to be here. What if she was? "So what else do you know about me?"

The man grinned. "I know that your name is Grace Lewis, and you're moving here from Louisiana, which was a little strange to me. Shelby Springs is barely a dot on the map, but Pastor Judson said you found us through the church's social media page, which had exactly three posts on it this year, and heard we were looking for a church secretary. And I know that you're staying at the Gibson's guest house at least for a few weeks."

Grace's mind raced. Of course it was just a mix-up. Another woman named Grace should be arriving here today, but should she tell him he had the wrong girl? She cleared her throat as she made a decision. "Well, you certainly know a few things. But I don't know anything about you."

He reached out his hand to shake. "I'm Colton Macklin."

Grace gripped his hand as it engulfed her smaller one. She felt the calluses on his skin.

"My family owns a ranch here, and we've been a part of Shelby Springs Church for generations. I was just on my way there now. Pastor Judson wants to move some furniture in the office, and I offered to lend a hand."

"You're going to the church now?"

He flashed a smile, and Grace could have melted. His teeth were white against his tan skin, and his eyes lit up underneath his cowboy hat. "Like I said, I would be happy to give you a lift."

Grace swallowed to push down the fear surfacing. She couldn't say if she was more afraid of getting in the truck with this man she just met or of walking into the lie that she was the woman he thought she was. All she managed to say was, "Okay."

A few minutes later, she was sitting in the front seat of his pickup truck. She'd never ridden in a pickup truck before. Blaine drove a sports car that Grace had always thought was a little ridiculous. There was barely room for her and her purse, and the trunk only had enough room for a small bag or two. But Colton had lifted out the two suitcases and set them in the back end of the truck with no problem. She looked over at him now as they pulled onto the road.

He was already on the phone. "Hey, Nate," he said. "How's it going?"

Grace could hear the man on the other end of the phone talking. There were a few minutes of conversation, as if Colton had nowhere else to be. Life must move more slowly here.

"I have a situation," Colton finally said. "Need you to tow a car from Highway 72, over by the water tower." He paused as the man responded and then chuckled. "No, not my truck. You know this thing is in mint condition. It's a dark-blue BMW. Our new church secretary broke down on her way into town this morning. I'm taking her to the church now, but can you tow it to Alex's Garage? Just tell him to call me about it later, and we'll work out the details."

Grace listened and wondered if she would have enough cash to pay for the car repairs. Was this all a terrible idea? She could have just told him she wasn't the Grace moving here to work for the church. But she needed him to help her. She could start the job and stay until she could get her car fixed and save up a little money. Then she could move on.

"It's all set," Colton said, interrupting her thoughts. He had set the phone down and looked at her as he spoke.

"Thanks," she said. "I hope it's not too much trouble."

"Not at all. Nate's a buddy of mine, and Alex and I went to school together. They'll take good care of it."

"Okay." It seemed like a lame thing to say, but she didn't have any other words. What did you say to a man who rescued you from the side of the road and handed you a new life without even knowing he was doing it? She leaned back in her seat and watched out the window. They seemed to be coming into the main part of town now. All they had passed for a few miles was land, a few houses, and cows.

It wasn't much, but they drove past a row of shops, a feed and seed store, and what looked like a small diner. A few people stood outside on the sidewalk talking with one another. They looked like they were in no hurry to leave. Past the stores off to the left, the church came into view. Grace gazed up at the tall steeple on the brick building that looked older than her grandparents. It looked well kept, though, and the lawn out front was immaculate.

Colton pulled around to the back and parked in the lot close to the building. A small sign reading "Office" was positioned over a white door. "Here we are," he said.

Grace's heart galloped ahead as she swallowed. She should tell him now. There's been a mistake, she told herself to say, but nothing came out. Grace knew as soon as she stepped through that door, it would be too late. Did they know what this other Grace looked like? Would she be found out in just a few moments? That might be a relief. She would have to admit the confusion and not let things go any further.

She climbed down from the truck and glanced around. This town seemed like a nice place. Certainly, the people were friendly. It might be just the place to settle down, and Blaine wouldn't be able to find her in a small town in the middle of nowhere. Taking quick steps to keep up with his long strides, she followed Colton to the door and made her decision.

Colton held the door open for her and then walked

through. Grace stepped into a small foyer. There was a chair oddly situated in the middle of the floor and a bookcase on its side.

"Knock, knock," Colton's voice boomed as he called out.

"Back here," came a quiet reply from somewhere down the hallway.

Grace followed Colton down a narrow hallway. It was plain but clean. The walls held photographs of groups of people with their arms around each other, smiling. Some of them were black-and-white and faded to a point where she could barely see the people.

"Hey, Pastor Judson," Colton said, walking into a room at the back. "I found a new church secretary stranded on the side of the road."

Grace moved closer just as the man looked up from where he sat behind an old wooden desk.

"Oh my!" Pastor Judson said. "Are you Grace?"

She held her breath as she nodded quickly. Did she look like the woman he was expecting?

"And you've had trouble in town already?"

Grace waved a hand in the air. "I'm fine. Colton had my car towed and everything. I'm sure it will be fine."

"I'm so sorry about that. But we're so glad you're here now." Pastor Judson stood and reached out to take both of her hands in his. "It's so nice to put a face to the name, after only speaking over the phone."

Grace forced a smile. "Yes, it is so nice to meet you in person." She breathed a sigh of relief.

"I'm sorry things are such a mess here." He held his arms out, indicating the disarray of the office. "But we weren't expecting you for a few more days. Colton was coming by to help me get things all rearranged."

"Oh, well, that's no problem. I, um, I just decided to go ahead and get out of town. You know, just eager to get started somewhere new." There, that was true. She didn't have to pile lies on top of each other.

Pastor Judson grinned. "We're happy to have you. It's still surprising to me that you wanted to come here. But after reading your letter and talking to you for a short time, I felt like The Lord had a hand in you coming here. I know He has a wonderful plan for you."

Grace's heart flip-flopped. She had heard those words before, but she had pushed them away. If God had a plan for her, He certainly had a roundabout way of getting to it. "Thank you for having me," she managed to say.

"Well, I hope you're not too eager to get to work. Why don't you take a few days just getting to know the place, and we'll have everything set up for you to start on Monday."

"Sure, sounds good to me."

"Are the Gibson's ready for you?"

"Oh, I don't know. They probably aren't expecting me just yet. I'm afraid I didn't think this through very well." Another wave of panic gripped at her heart. What if the Gibson's knew more about the other Grace?

"I'm sure they're all ready," Colton said. "I saw Mrs. Gibson at the store just yesterday. She told me her niece left a few days ago, and she was just putting the finishing touches on the guest house."

"Well, then, it sounds like everything is all set. Grace, I'll introduce you to the congregation on Sunday morning during the service, if that's all right."

"Of course."

He grinned. "Although I'm sure by then you'll know half of them." He waved a hand in the air. "No matter. Colton, can you help Grace get to the Gibson's? Our furniture moving can wait just a bit longer."

"Yes, sir. I'll be back soon." With that he turned and walked back down the hallway and waited for Grace to follow him as he held the door open.

"Thank you," she said quietly as she walked toward his truck. Now she had a job, a place to stay, and a town where she might get along without her car for a few days at least.

The only question was, what in the world had she gotten herself into?

2

olton was quiet as he drove up the driveway to his parents' house. The morning had been nothing like he had expected. Did he really pick up a woman on the side of the road? That kind of thing didn't happen to normal people like him. Especially the youngest brother who no one thought was capable of doing anything.

But it had happened. Colton's mind went to the woman, and he wondered what Grace was doing now. He had taken her to the Gibson's house. Mrs. Gibson was thrilled to have her there earlier than expected, and he'd carried her luggage to the front door of the guest house. He didn't feel he should intrude further. He had already been closer to this total stranger than he would have under any normal circumstances. He lifted his hand in a wave as he turned to go. What was that look on her face? Confusion? Fear? Her eyes darted back and forth quickly as if she were waiting for something to go wrong.

Colton couldn't linger in the moment, but she had

remained on his mind, and he wondered what her story was. What kind of person took a job and moved to a town where she knew no one and started over? He wouldn't know anything about that; he had lived in the same house since he came home from the hospital as a baby.

He climbed from his truck and made his way up the steps to the front door. The screen door creaked in the old familiar way as he opened it. Voices echoed through the house, and he knew his brothers had gathered for lunch. Colton grimaced at the prospect of eating with them today. Why hadn't he gotten something to eat in town before he came back?

Anybody in town could probably answer that. Because Lydia Macklin was the best cook in town. Even if Colton wanted to avoid his brothers, the food was worth it.

His boots thudded across the wood floor as he made his way through the house into the large dining room where everyone was already seated at the table with plates of food.

"Hey, Colt," Sawyer said from his seat. "We were just wondering where you were."

Colton scoffed. "Yeah, right."

"It's true," Jenson said around the bite of food in his mouth.

"Why? Did you actually notice that it was harder to get the work done without me?"

"Nah," Jenson said, a teasing look in his eyes. "We were just talking about that time when we were kids and you fell in the creek in December."

Colton narrowed his eyes at the memory. "It wasn't that cold."

Sawyer laughed. "I think Mom has a picture of you coming back to the house soaking wet."

"It wouldn't have happened if y'all hadn't gone off and left me."

Sawyer turned to his wife. "He was only about six. We told him he was too little and to stay at the house, but he didn't listen."

Katie swatted her husband's arm before putting her hand to her pregnant belly. "I can't believe you would do that to him."

"See?" Colton said. "It wasn't my fault."

"That's right," Katie nodded. "You're supposed to look after your baby brother."

Colton ignored the last remark and went to the counter to fix himself a plate. After piling a generous serving of cilantro chicken and rice on his plate, he made his way back to the table and took a seat at the end. "I could take care of myself, but you took the board with you, and I had to go across the tree limb hanging over the water.

"I guess you were big enough to break the limb."

"He's lucky he didn't break and arm…or his neck," Lydia Macklin said of her youngest son. "But he's right. It wasn't a very cold winter. He survived."

"I've survived a lot in this family."

"That's true," Sawyer said. "Speaking of, I want to say thanks to everyone for offering to help out so I can take some time off when the baby comes. It means a lot to me."

"I haven't heard about these arrangements," Dad said. "What can I do to help?"

"Lawson's got it all under control," Sawyer said. "No need to worry."

Colton kept his head down as he ate his food. No need to worry. The older brothers would handle it like always, and he would keep on doing what he always did. Even if they didn't notice.

GRACE SAT ON THE EDGE OF THE BED AND TOOK IN THE room. The guest house was small but nice. Mrs. Gibson had greeted them in the driveway after Colton called to say they were on their way. Grace was shocked when the woman pulled her into a hug as if they were old friends who hadn't seen each other in years.

The guest house was steps away from the main house and had a tiny kitchen and one bedroom and bath. She knew her mother would just die at the size of it. She had always told Grace to expect the best and she could be the best. But Grace didn't mind the house. It felt cozy and manageable.

Now it was dark, and she stared at her suitcases that she had dragged into the room. It felt strange to unpack them. That would mean she was really staying, and right now she was still sure that someone was going to burst in the room any minute and call her out for her lie.

"God," she whispered as she squeezed her eyes closed, "I don't know what I'm doing here. I'm sorry that I let them think I was the other Grace, but I don't have anywhere else to go. This seems as good of a place as any, and everyone has been so nice. Could you maybe make it so I can stay? I don't know how, and if it doesn't work, I know it's my fault anyway." She stopped then and sighed.

Of course, she couldn't stay. But maybe she could enjoy it while it lasted.

Still, she didn't see any reason to unpack those suitcases.

The next morning, the sun shone right in through the white linen curtains. Grace stretched her arms above her head as she yawned. Her stomach grumbled right at that moment, and she remembered that she had no food in the house and no car to get anywhere. Maybe Mrs. Gibson had left some food in the cabinets, but probably not. It wasn't her job to feed her. Grace tossed back the covers and stepped down onto the hardwood floors. As she padded to the kitchen, she thanked The Lord that the other Grace had managed to secure a furnished rental. She sure would look funny coming into town with no furniture and sleeping on the floor.

Just as she started to look through the cabinets, a knock sounded at the door. She jumped at the sound. Had Blaine found her? Or was it Mrs. Gibson coming to kick her out?

Grace took quick steps to the bedroom and grabbed her robe and slipped it on before making her way to the door. She took a deep breath and blew it out before she opened the door just a crack.

"Morning." Colton stood on the porch.

"Hey," Grace said, just peeking her face out. It was far enough to get a good look at the man. He wore jeans and a T-shirt and his cowboy hat. Somehow, the sight of him made her feel a little at ease. He looked calm and comfortable and not at all like he was here to drive her out of town.

"Sorry to come by so early."

"Oh that's all right. I was up."

"I brought your car."

"Really?" Grace forgot her state of dress and flung the door open to step out and see her vehicle sitting in the driveway. "Wow! That was fast."

Colton stepped back and seemed to take her in. "Um, yeah. Well, Alex finished it up last night. Said the fuel pump was bad."

"And you went to get it? I could have done that." She didn't know how, but it felt like the right thing to say. "Besides, I didn't even pay for it yet."

"That's all right. I told him you were the new church secretary, and he could trust you."

Grace looked up to meet his eyes and swallowed hard. She wished he could trust her. But Colton was wrong about her. "Thanks," she managed to say. "I can pay you for your time. I know you have other things to do than take care of my business for me."

Colton grinned. Grace could have melted on the spot at that look. "We like to take care of people around here. You'll get used to it."

"Well, thanks. Maybe I can return the favor sometime."

Colton put his hands on his hips. "You could drive me back to the garage to get my truck."

Grace's hand flew to her mouth. "Oh, of course. I'm sorry. Let me just get dressed." She turned before looking at him and ran back in the house, shutting the door behind her. She shut herself in the bedroom and grabbed for her suitcase. The first thing she found was a pair of jeans and a T-shirt. They were both a couple of years old, but they looked brand new, since she couldn't remember when she had actually worn them. Blaine liked for her to be more dressed up, and he hated T-shirts.

For just a second, she wondered what Colton would think about her in jeans and a T-shirt. But she brushed that thought away as quickly as it had come. She couldn't be thinking about him like that. He was here to help her because people here were friendly, not any other reason. Besides, if he found out she wasn't who she was pretending to be, he wouldn't want anything to do with her.

No, she couldn't get attached to anyone here. She just needed to stay safe and off the radar. At least until she was sure Blaine wasn't going to come after her. Then she could move on.

Grace grabbed her purse and ran back out the front door.

"Ready?" Colton asked as she brushed past him.

"Yep, let's do it." Grace determined not to look at him as she walked to the car. He was too good-looking for her to watch him and walk at the same time. She needed to focus.

Colton walked to the passenger side and climbed in at the same time that she got into the driver's seat. Her car suddenly felt tiny with the tall man sitting beside her. He had to be over six feet. He slipped his hat off and set it in his lap, and she noticed his light-brown hair for the first time.

Nope. Don't even think about it. She cranked the car and pulled out of the driveway before she stopped and looked at him. "I'm sorry. I just realized I have no idea where we're going."

Colton chuckled, and the corners of his mouth lifted

into a crooked smile. "Turn right. I'll walk you through it. It's not far."

Grace glanced at him out of the corner of her eye. With that grin and those eyes sitting next to her, she wondered if she would remember where to turn if she had been there a hundred times. She cleared her throat as she accelerated on the road. "So how long have you lived in Shelby Springs?"

"My whole life," he said. "My family owns a ranch, and we've been here for generations."

"Is that what you do? Work at the ranch?"

"Yep. Our whole family works it together."

"So you're like a real cowboy then?"

"Yes, ma'am."

"Wow. I, uh, I've never met a real cowboy. So, like, you ride a horse and chase cows and everything?"

"Wrangle cows. I don't usually chase them. But yep, sure do. I've been riding a horse since before I could walk."

"That's nice," Grace said. It was different, that was for sure. She'd never been on a ranch, and her father wore suits to work every day, and Blaine did the same.

"Have you ever ridden a horse?" Colton asked.

"Oh no, not me. I'm a city girl. Grew up in a neighborhood with one strip of grass. Probably the farthest thing possible from a ranch."

"But you decided to move to Texas?"

Grace's eyes widened as she tried to force a smile. "I, uh, I was just ready for a change. I guess if you want change, going somewhere completely different is a good idea."

Colton rubbed his chin. "I guess so. Honestly, I've never thought about leaving, so I wouldn't know."

"You're pretty happy with your life then?"

His eyes narrowed, and he seemed to carefully weigh his words. "It's not perfect. There are some things I wish I could change, but I do want to live here and work here."

Grace wondered if she should push him, but the words tumbled out before she could stop them. "What would you change?"

He took a deep breath and blew it out. "Let's just say being the youngest of seven brothers is a challenge."

"Seven?" Grace shouted, her voice echoing in the small car.

"Yep. I'm number seven, with six older brothers."

"Wow," Grace said. "I don't know anyone who has that many siblings. And no girls?"

"Nope. I do have two sisters-in-law now, but that's it."

"I guess that's good for a ranching family, lots of strong arms to do the work." Were all his brothers that fit and handsome?

"It is. The ranch couldn't run without a lot of hands."

"But you don't like being the youngest."

"I don't like being treated like a baby."

Grace couldn't imagine anyone treating the man beside her like a baby. He certainly looked capable. "I'm sorry. I know something about what that's like. My family has always tried to plan out my life for me, as if I couldn't make my own decisions."

Colton nodded as if he understood, but didn't say any more about it. "Turn here." He pointed to a road on the right, and Grace took the turn.

Only a moment later, Colton pointed out another turn, and then they were in the parking lot of the garage.

Grace slowly climbed out of the car, following Colton's lead as he made his way into the building." Hey, man," Colton said to the man behind the counter. "This is Grace."

Grace looked at the man with his backward baseball cap, collared shirt, and jeans. "Hi, it's nice to meet you. Thank you so much for helping with my car. Wasn't sure what I was going to do."

"Aw, it was nothing," said the man. "We're always happy to help out. Especially a friend of the Macklin family. "

Grace glanced over at Colton. What would it be like to actually be a friend of the Macklin family, or more specifically, of Colton's? Not that it was possible now, since he didn't know who she really was. She forced a smile. "Well, thanks. It sure is nice to feel welcome in this town. I'd like to settle up my bill."

Alex gave her the total, and she pulled out the amount in cash, whispering a prayer of thanks that she had enough to cover it. She wondered when she would get a paycheck from her new job, but it felt wrong to ask, since the other Grace probably knew those kinds of details. She turned to Colton. "Thanks again for all your help. I'm sure you need to get back to work at the ranch."

Colton tugged on his cowboy hat. "Yeah, as a matter of fact, I do. But I'm happy to see that you're doing all right and that you're back on your feet with your car."

Grace was surprised that she felt sad for him to go. But then again, she didn't know anyone else in town. Of course she would feel sad the only person she knew would be leaving her again. What in the world would she do all day? In a town she knew nothing about?

As if he'd read her mind, Colton spoke up as they walked across the parking lot. "Do you have plans for the day?"

She turned her palms to the sky and shrugged. "Not really. Just getting to know the town I guess."

"You should eat lunch at the diner. It will be busy on Saturday, and you're bound to meet people. Everyone is excited to meet the new church secretary."

A lump formed in Grace's stomach at the thought of that. Of course she would have to meet people, but who would be the person to rat her out? "That sounds nice," she lied.

"It won't take you long to tour the place. If you start at one end of Main Street, you could make it to the other end in no time." He chuckled.

"I could make my way in some of the stores. Is there a coffee shop?" she asked.

He nodded. "It's a bakery, but they sell coffee. I guess it's good. I wouldn't know. I drink coffee at home."

Grace grinned. "I bet you do."

"Well, I do need to get going." He handed her a piece of paper he pulled from his pocket. "Here's my number if you need anything. Please feel free to call." With that, he touched the brim of his hat, turned, and climbed in his truck.

Grace turned away too, resisting the urge to watch him until he was out of sight. Once she was alone again, she climbed into her car and started to drive. Just like the day she arrived, she didn't know where she was going, only that she needed to be moving. Her stomach grumbled, reminding her she still hadn't eaten. Where was that bakery Colton had mentioned? She made her way to Main Street and parked when she saw the sign above the shop. The clear glass windows displayed cakes, cupcakes, and pastries of various kinds.

She climbed out and slung her purse over her shoulder. Looking up and down the street, she saw only a few cars and a handful of people. Colton said there would be a lot of people at the diner for lunch. Maybe before that people were at home doing ranch chores or sitting on their porch sipping their own coffee.

Grace opened the door of the bakery and a tiny bell jingled overhead.

"Good mornin'," called out a voice. "Be right with ya."

Grace stepped inside and inhaled deeply. The scent of cinnamon hung in the air, making her even hungrier.

"Hi there." A woman who looked to be in her early fifties stepped through the back doorway wiping her hands on her apron. "What can I get you?" She eyed Grace as if she had so many questions and that wasn't the one she wanted to ask.

"I'd like a coffee, and what's your most popular muffin?"

"Hmm." The woman tapped her chin with her index finger. "This week I would say the cinnamon spice muffin, but the apple cinnamon is always popular too."

"I'll take one of each then," Grace said.

"Sure thing. You want cream in your coffee? I can do a latte?"

"Oh, a vanilla latte would be wonderful." Grace hadn't dared to ask for anything fancy. The shop looked nice, but she didn't want to assume they could do the same as the coffee shop back home.

"Coming right up." The woman smiled. She turned and continued to chat while she went to work. "I'm Janelle, by the way. This is my place."

"It's lovely," Grace said.

"Are you passing through?"

Here we go. "Actually, I'm new in town. I'm Grace, the new church secretary."

"Is that so?" Janelle turned to look her over. "Well then, welcome to Shelby Springs."

"Thank you." Grace nodded. "Happy to be here." So far anyway. She did like what she'd seen, and it made her wish she was the Grace they had been expecting and she could stay.

Janelle made quick work of fixing the coffee and slipping several muffins in the bag.

Grace reached for her wallet, but Janell held up her hand. "No charge. It'll be a little welcome gift. I hope you'll be back for more."

"I'm sure I will."

"So where is it you came here from?"

Grace swallowed. "Louisiana."

"That's right, I heard that somewhere," Janelle said. "And you're single I guess."

Grace nodded slowly. She hadn't thought about it like that, but she guessed she finally was. All that time trying to break up with Blaine and go about her normal life, and now she was rid of him, but in a way she'd never expected.

"Well, there's plenty of eligible bachelors around town.

If you don't mind 'em smelling like horses that is." Janelle laughed.

Grace smiled. "I'm not looking for a relationship anyway. Just a fresh start."

Janelle looked thoughtful as she leaned against the counter. "Sometimes we're not ready for another person to be part of our lives until we get our fresh start. Once we get on our own two feet and figure out life a little, then we realize we're ready to share it."

Grace stared at the woman. What a thing to say to a total stranger. Grace had no response. "Thank you for the muffins, and the coffee. I'm sure I'll see you around."

"Sure thing. I'll see you at church tomorrow."

Grace nodded. "Yes, I'll be there." She backed out the door with her coffee and bag of muffins. She walked straight to her car where she could eat and sip the hot beverage in silence. After one interaction, she'd lost her nerve at meeting the townsfolk. And she'd already promised to be at church tomorrow. How in the world was she going to face all those people and keep pretending this was where she planned to be?

3

*C*olton turned up the driveway to Whispering Oaks Ranch. He could remember the first time he'd driven this road in the old beat up work truck they kept on the ranch. At sixteen, it was practically a Macklin law that you drive that dirty, smelly truck for the first year. Of course, by the time Colton drove it, it had been through six brothers first. Hand-me-downs were a way of life for him. It wasn't always so bad really. When he was a kid he thought it was cool to have something one of his brothers wore. He looked up to them and wanted to be just like them anyway. But as a teenager, he would grit his teeth every time one of them would say, "Hey, I remember that shirt. I wore it all the time."

Now, he bought his own clothes and his own truck. He had saved up until he could buy the exact model he wanted. It wasn't brand new—Dad had taught him the value of buying a used vehicle—but it was clean and nice, and the deep-blue pickup truck was the exact color he had imagined. His brothers teased him over how meticulously he cleaned a truck that was driven around a cattle ranch, but he was proud to have it, and he would wash it every day if he needed to.

He parked in his designated spot in the yard in front of the big house and jumped out.

"Morning," Lawson called out from the porch. "Late start today?" he asked, lifting his cup of coffee in the air. "We've already eaten breakfast."

Colton scowled. "No, early start. I ate before I left, and I've already been in town. Headed to the barn now."

"Gotcha. I'm leaving for an auction in Austin that's this afternoon. You sure you don't want to tag along? I'm happy to teach you if you want to take over the buying and selling."

"No thanks. I don't need your job."

Lawson shrugged. "Suit yourself. Just thought you wanted to be helpful. Since I'm taking over other responsibilities, you know."

"Yeah, yeah, I know. But I guess you can handle it without me."

Lawson started to say something else, but Colton didn't hear it. His feet pounded the ground at a quick pace toward the barn. He would check on the herd in the north pasture to get his day started. Whatever his brothers said, he was the hardest worker on this ranch.

***

Monday morning, Grace sat in her car in the parking lot of the church. She was early and hadn't been able to convince herself to go inside. Church the day before had been exciting and terrifying. Everyone was so kind and welcoming. It felt wonderful. And terrible. She loved how they made her a part of the community on day one, but the fact that it wasn't supposed to be her gnawed at her insides.

She swallowed hard to push down the rising fear and stepped out of the car. Pastor Judson's car was there, and she assumed he was already inside. It was time to get moving. She jutted her chin in the air and promised herself she could do this.

As soon as she opened the front door she heard, "Good morning, Grace."

"Good morning, Pastor Judson," she said, closing the door behind her.

"How was your first weekend in Shelby Springs?"

"It was very nice," she said. It was true. If she were the real Grace, she would have enjoyed every second of it.

"I'm glad to hear it. When I first came here, I wasn't sure what to expect. I had been called down from a church just outside of Dallas. But a second cousin of mine lived in Shelby Springs, and when the pastor retired, she recommended me for the job. I'll be honest, I had imagined myself pastoring a church that was growing in a bigger town. But once I got here, I knew I was home. This town is exactly where God wanted me to be, even if I didn't know it myself."

Grace smiled. "That must be nice."

"Yes, it is." Pastor Judson smiled back. "But you decided to make this your home without even seeing it first."

Grace gave a nervous laugh. "Yes, I guess I did."

"And we're glad you did. So are you ready to get started for your first day?"

"Absolutely."

Pastor Judson clapped his hands together. "Great. Colton and I got the furniture rearranged, so this will be your work space." He held out his hands and indicated the desk and chair. "I know it's not much, but I hope it will do."

"It looks great to me."

"You'll be responsible for answering the phone. I don't mind taking calls if someone needs to speak with me, but obviously if I'm in a meeting or out of the office, you can take a message, and if you feel it's urgent, you can call my cell phone. One thing that's very important to your position is keeping things in confidence. You might see someone come in for counseling, or hear conversations of a sensitive nature. Especially because we live in a small town, we want to respect people's privacy, so it's extremely important that you keep these things to yourself."

Grace nodded. "I understand." She was pretty sure she could keep a secret.

"Well then, now that's out of the way, let me show you the always exciting copier and supplies room."

Pastor Judson spent the next hour going over Grace's responsibilities at the church. In addition to answering phones, she would handle the church calendar, coordinate with various volunteers for ministries, and format and print the weekly bulletin for Sunday morning. Grace felt confident that she could handle the tasks, although she had almost no experience using a copier. She hoped she could fake it until she figured it out.

"Any questions?" Pastor Judson asked as they walked back to Grace's desk.

"No, I don't think so."

"Well, if you think of anything, I'm just down the hall in my office. I know it will take some time to settle in, so let me know how I can help."

"Thanks," Grace said. "I will."

Pastor Judson headed for his own office, and Grace took a seat at the desk. She had just leaned her head back on the chair and was taking a deep breath when the phone rang. She startled and sat straight up.

"Here goes nothing," she said. She picked up the phone. "Shelby Springs Community Church."

"Hi, this is Grace Lewis."

Grace froze. Here it was. The moment everything would come crashing down. She felt like she should say something, but no words came out.

"I'm supposed to be there this morning to start work."

Grace swallowed hard and managed to squeak out, "Yes."

"I'm so sorry. My plans have changed. My grandmother who lives in Florida had a stroke, and I have to go and stay with her. It looks like it could be a long recovery, so I don't know when or if I would be able to come."

"Oh that's all right. Of course you need to take care of her."

"Please tell Pastor Judson I'm sorry. I was so looking forward to living in Shelby Springs, but God must have other plans."

Grace couldn't believe what she was hearing. She sat in stunned silence for several seconds before she finally spoke. "Yes, yes, I guess He does. Thank you for letting us know. I'll say a prayer for your grandmother."

"Oh thank you so much. I need to go now. Have a wonderful day."

With that, the other Grace was gone.

She wouldn't be showing up to expose Grace, she was never coming, and Grace could stay in Shelby Springs and fall right into this life. Maybe this was where she was supposed to be after all.

4

Colton dragged himself out of his truck and gripped the picnic basket he held with both hands. What had his mother packed that was so doggone heavy? Not that it mattered. Everyone would know that the food was good. He cringed at the thought of the event.

"Hey there, bachelor number four," Pastor Judson said.

Colton rolled his eyes. "I've definitely never been called that before." Colton stopped and reached out to shake hands, balancing the basket on the ground so he didn't drop it.

Pastor Judson laughed. "We're just grateful to everyone for helping out and donating their time."

"It's only slightly embarrassing."

"Now don't worry about that. I'm sure all the ladies will want to bid on the man that goes with that basket."

"All for a good cause, right?" Colton said, trying not to wince.

"That's right. The elementary school fundraiser is a wonderful cause." Pastor Judson smiled. "I'll see you later."

Colton touched the brim of his cowboy hat as he watched the other man pick up the pace and move toward the pavilion. His phone vibrated in his pocket, and he reached for it. A text from Mom read: *Good luck! I'm sure there will be plenty of bids. I know of at least one in particular.*

Inwardly, he groaned. Mom must have been encouraging one of the local girls to bid on him for a date. He didn't need any help there. He could find his own woman, if he wanted one. Couldn't he? There were a couple of girls in town he could ask out anytime he wanted. That was true, wasn't it?

"Hey, Colton."

He turned at the sound of a female voice. "Oh hi, Grace." He looked at her as if for the first time. She wore a white sundress that set off the tan color of her skin. Her dark hair fell in waves around her shoulders. "How are you?" he asked.

"I'm good. A little excited to see the festivities today. I've never been to a bachelor auction fundraiser before. It sounds thrilling." She paused, and her eyes grew wide. "To watch, I mean."

"Oh you're just planning to watch?"

She shrugged. "Yes. I don't really know anyone here that well. Are there other items to bid on? You know, I mean, besides….men?" Her cheeks flushed pink.

It was adorable. "There are a number of other items, donated by some of the local business owners. I think Sierra donated a month of riding lessons, Mom has a couple of her cakes, and Garrett is auctioning a couple of his leather projects."

"Wow, sounds like your family is doing their part." She

pointed at the basket. "Does that mean you're in the auction?"

Colton sighed and nodded. "Yep."

"Are your other brothers in it too?"

"Nope. Just me. Every year one of us does it. I drew the short straw this time."

"Oh?" Grace raised her eyebrows. "You didn't volunteer with excitement to stand in front of the whole town and have women bid to spend time with you?" Her eyes twinkled.

"Well, since you put it that way…" He smiled. "No, I didn't. I'm glad to help with the fundraiser, but it's embarrassing, not to mention the awkward lunch afterward. Especially since I think my mom has someone she is trying to set me up with."

"Oh, that *is* awkward. I know something about being set up by your parents." She bit her lip, and her eyes darted back and forth.

"Did they have someone for you back in Louisiana?"

Grace nodded but didn't make eye contact. She cleared her throat. "I went out with him for a while. I wanted to end things with him, but every time I tried, my parents would push us back together."

"I'm sorry."

Grace shrugged and pasted on a smile. "Anyway, that's behind me. So who do you think your mom is trying to set you up with?" She looked around as if she might see the woman walking by.

"I'm not sure. There are a couple girls that I went to high school with that she mentions from time to time. She just wants all of us married and settled. But I think I would rather meet someone on my own than have my mom get someone to bid on me."

Grace smiled. "I understand."

Colton looked at her and had an idea. "I know you said you're not planning to bid, but umm." He took his hat off and rubbed the back of his neck. "You know, just to protect me from whoever my mom has in mind, do you think you could bid on me?"

Grace's eyes flew open wide. "Oh, I, umm."

He held his hands up. "No pressure. But I would even pay for it. I don't mind. And everyone here will tell you, all the food in this basket is made by my mom. She's the best cook in town."

Grace smiled. "Well, maybe just for the food."

"Sure. You can have the whole basket. Besides, I certainly wouldn't mind running up the bid. My brothers have been the highest bid winners the last four years. It would be something to get more than them."

Grace crossed her arms in front of her and bit her lip as if she were considering it. "All right," she finally said, "I'll do it."

Colton let out a sigh of relief. "Perfect." He reached down and lifted the heavy basket. "I've got to get this up to the table. I guess I'll see you up there."

Colton walked away, taking silent deep breaths. Did he really just do that? Asked a woman to bid on him? That might be a new low. Sure, he said it was to avoid other unwanted bids, but was that the whole truth? Truthfully, he wanted an excuse to get to know her better. The fact that she up and left her home to move to a town where she knew no one intrigued him. If he was telling the whole story, he would have to admit that he had lain awake at night wondering what made her do that. Now he wondered if it had to do with the man her parents tried to force on her. Would he ever get so fed up with his family that he would move away?

He shook his head as he lifted the basket to set it on the auction table. He needed to push those thoughts aside. Shelby Springs was home, and Whispering Oaks Ranch was in his blood. He could never leave.

But he wanted to know more about the woman who walked away from her home for a new life. Maybe this was his chance.

Colton mingled around as the townsfolk gathered in the square. He remembered attending events here as a kid. Back then he thought it was fun just to come and play with his friends as they ran in the grass. Life had been simpler then, but he could remember watching as the grownups walked hand-in-hand or sat on blankets together to eat a picnic lunch. He couldn't wait to grow up and be a dad. Then he could be in charge of himself. These days he wondered if he would ever feel like a grown-up.

"Hey, Colt," Sawyer called out from where the family was gathered.

Colton lifted his hand as he moved toward them.

"Here's our man," Lawson said, patting him in the shoulder. "Ready to represent the clan? Think you can beat my record from last year?"

Colton gave a wry smile. "Let's just wait and see."

"Ladies and gentlemen," Mayor Kenton came over the speakers, "we're so grateful that you're all here today. Welcome to the fifteenth annual Shelby Springs Elementary Fundraiser Auction! We have a number of great items up for bid today, culminating in our popular bachelor picnic auction. I've peeked in some of those baskets, and let me tell you, ladies, I hope you're hungry because they look delicious."

As people gathered to stand near the pavilion, they clapped and cheered.

"My lovely wife will be helping us. Dear, what's the first item we have?"

Mrs. Kenton held up a large envelope and spoke into the microphone. "A month of horseback riding lessons with Sierra Macklin at Whispering Oaks Ranch."

"Wonderful," Mayor Finch said. "Let's start the bidding."

Colton's head whipped back and forth, watching the audience bid and outbid each other. It went so fast, but in a matter of minutes, the first item was sold. The Macklin family cheered and hugged Sierra.

The bidding continued, and they watched as the diner auctioned free dinners for a month, and Sawyer even bid on a weeklong vacation to the beach.

"What would you do at the beach?" Jenson asked him.

Sawyer tugged on his cowboy hat as he said, "Watch the first waves from the window."

Everyone laughed.

"Yeah, right. Like you would take a whole week off of work," Lawson said.

"He will when this little one arrives," Katie said, rubbing her belly.

"Yes, he most certainly will," Lydia Macklin said of her oldest son. She gave Katie a squeeze. "And we just can't wait for that day!"

Katie sucked in a breath and made a face as she blew it out. "Me either. I feel like a whale."

"Not at all," Sawyer said, kissing her cheek. "You look beautiful."

"Hey, Mom's recipes are up," Hawk said.

Lydia covered her face with her hands, but her family cheered as the price for the recipes went up and up.

When all the items on the table were gone, Colton sucked in a breath as the Mayor moved on to the picnic baskets.

"Now, most of you know, but for any newcomers, we have a little tradition here with the auctioning of these picnic baskets. Each basket has been prepared by one of our town's eligible bachelors."

A few women in the crowd cheered and one let out a high-pitched whistle.

The mayor laughed. "Yes, yes, I know you're excited. So each of these baskets will be auctioned, and with it comes the company of the man who packed it for a picnic lunch. Now, you're welcome to bid on the man you think is the best looking, or the basket that looks the most delicious. And remember, this is for the school and all in good fun." The mayor clapped his hands together. "Let's get started."

Colton watched as the bidding began for the first basket. It looked like a tiny lunch. Definitely not enough food for a Macklin man. Still a couple of teenage girls went back and forth, increasing the bid one dollar at a time. Colton smiled when he saw the teenage boy who had brought the basket blushing and grinning from ear to ear. He went for nineteen dollars and fifteen cents and looked pleased as punch.

The next basket went for seventy-five dollars, and the one after that for eighty. Colton could see that things were warming up, and his basket was next in line.

"Now, I can see here this is the Macklin basket." The mayor tried to lift it and set it back down. "It's definitely full. I imagine that there's one of Lydia Macklin's famous pies in there too, and it comes with the company of Mr. Colton Macklin. Let's start the bidding at twenty-five dollars."

Colton took a deep breath as Sawyer patted him on the shoulder.

"Just remember," Garrett said, "I hold the record at two twenty-five."

"Yeah, you haven't let us forget it," Jenson said.

Colton glanced over and saw Grace standing at the edge of the crowd. He shouldn't have asked her to do this. She was brand new in town and didn't need everyone thinking she was chasing him. His insides warmed at the thought of her being interested in him. That wouldn't be bad at all. But she couldn't be; she didn't even know him.

The mayor was raising the bid ten dollars at a time, and in no time he was up to one hundred dollars. That was good, but it needed to keep going if he was going to beat his brothers.

"Do I hear one hundred twenty-five?" The mayor asked.

From the back of the crowd, Colton heard a voice answer, "One hundred twenty-five." He turned to look, and his eyes grew wide.

"Colt, isn't that..." Sawyer said but didn't finish the thought.

Colton nodded and looked away quickly. "Yep," he said.

"I thought she moved away," Lawson said.

"She did, but her parents still live here."

Lydia smiled. "Oh, I heard Susan was in town this weekend. I told her mother we would look forward to seeing her."

Great. Susan Nevins was still chasing him. He had been out with her a couple of times in high school. Mostly because his mother thought she was a nice girl and kept pushing him to spend time with her. But Colton didn't like how she threw herself at him and on the first date acted like they were an established couple making plans for the future. No, he did not want Susan Nevins to win the bid on his basket. He had been relieved when she moved away and had no desire to rekindle any kind of relationship over a picnic lunch.

"One fifty," he heard another voice say.

Colton smiled as he saw Grace raise her hand. She would save him.

"One seventy-five," Susan said.

"Two hundred," Grace countered.

Colton watched as Susan blinked rapidly and seemed to consider this. "Two twenty-five," she said."

"Two fifty," Grace said, lifting her chin in the air.

Susan scowled and shook her head in defeat.

The mayor looked out over the crowd. "Two fifty going once, two fifty going twice, sold for two hundred and fifty dollars."

Sawyer cheered as he put both hands on Colton's shoulders and shook him. "Way to go, Colt!"

Jenson reached up and snatched Colton's cowboy hat off and ruffled his hair. "Good job, little brother."

Garret frowned but reached out to shake Colton's hand. "Congratulations."

"Thanks, bro."

"I guess you better go get your date." Sawyer winked.

Colton cleared his throat. "It's not a date. It's just lunch…for charity."

"Nah, I think it's a date," Jenson said.

Colton's heart picked up the pace. It wasn't really, was it? She had only agreed to help him. "I don't even know her," he said.

"That's the point of a date," Katie spoke up. "You eat a meal, and you get to know each other."

"Is that what a date is?" Sawyer asked, giving Katie a wink.

"Yes." She swatted his arm playfully. "It just so happens that I already knew I liked you before you asked me on a date."

"Gosh, Sawyer, didn't you know you're supposed to woo her with a fancy dinner?" Jenson teased.

"Look who's talking," Sierra said.

"That was different. It's hard to go on dates when you have two kids at home."

Sierra leaned over and kissed his cheek. "That's ok. Falling in love with you at a horse ranch is better than any fancy dinner."

Lydia gave Colton a gentle push. "Go on, son. She's waiting on you."

Colton's feet started moving before he was sure he was ready. But his mother was right. Grace stood at the front by the picnic basket he was sure was too heavy for her to pick up. The mayor had moved on to the next basket, so Colton hurried down front.

"Hey," he said, lifting the basket in a quick motion and continuing to walk. "I hope you're hungry."

"Seriously. What is in that thing?" Grace pointed at the basket.

"A three-course meal, I guess. I think she put bread, fried chicken, potato salad, and a chocolate pie for dessert."

"Oh, chocolate pie is my favorite," Grace said.

"Mine too."

They made their way to the field where kids were running and playing and some of the other couples from the basket auction were already setting up their lunches.

Colton set the basket down and opened it to pull out a large quilt. He spread it out and motioned for Grace to sit.

"This is a beautiful quilt," she said. "Did your mother make it?"

He shook his head. "My great-grandmother I think. But my mom does quilt. We've got a whole closet full of these things."

"That's amazing. I can't think of anything we have that was my great-grandmother's, and my mom doesn't make anything. She buys things online."

Colton chuckled. "My family's motto is 'why buy it when you can make it?' Although, sometimes, making it is more expensive."

"Maybe, but it means so much more. And I'm sure the quality is much better than store bought. I would love to know how to sew. I can't sew on a button."

"Well, I can teach you to do that. Macklin boys learn to sew a shirt button at the age of five. We're pretty rough on clothing on the ranch, but there's no reason to throw out a shirt because of a button or a tear. We grew up working in patched clothes. Especially me. All the hand-me-downs were rough by the time I got them."

Grace reached for the basket and peered in. "Wow, there's dishes and glasses in here. Your mom really thought of everything."

Colton nodded. "She's quite the hostess."

"And what about you? Is this the kind of thing you would plan for a date if you were doing it yourself?"

Colton felt his cheeks get hot. "I could plan it myself. And I could pack my own picnic too. My mom just does it because it's for charity and everyone is willing to pay top dollar for her cooking."

Grace dropped her gaze to the blanket. "I'm sorry, I didn't mean you couldn't. I was just curious what you do for your real dates."

"I know. Sorry, I didn't mean to snap. I'm just used to people thinking I'm the baby brother who can't do anything for himself."

Grace's eyes were wide as she snapped them back up to look at him. "I don't think that at all."

Colton smiled. "Let's change the subject. To answer your question, honestly, I haven't done much dating. A little bit in high school, but nothing serious."

"Really?" Grace said. "I'm surprised. It seems like girls here would fall all over you." She blushed as she realized what she had said. "I mean, um, your family just seems so well liked in town and everything."

"That's true. I just didn't want to be liked for my family. I'm a part of my family, and I'm proud of that. But I want to be liked for being my own person. It's just hard for anyone to see me behind the shadow of my brothers."

"Well, I want to know you. Who is Colton? Not Macklin, just Colton."

Colton didn't speak for a moment. He quietly handed Grace a plate and a fork, then laid out all the food on the blanket and sat back. He nodded for her to go ahead.

"Just Colton, huh? I guess I'm so used to being one of the Macklin brothers. I do love living on the ranch and working with the cattle. I've been a hard worker my whole life, so the early mornings and late evenings don't bother me. I like to be busy, and I like to be useful."

"But that's just what you do. What do you care about the most?"

Colton filled his own plate with food as he considered his answer. "People," he finally said. "I care about people and want them to have what they need and feel taken care of. I hate to see anyone go without. I guess that's why I work so hard. Our work provides cattle, and food, and now even work for other people. And we're fortunate enough to be part of a community here, and because of the ranch, we're able to help other people."

"Like with the auction today?"

He nodded. "Exactly. We are grateful for what we've been given, and we work hard for it, but we also know we should share and support others."

"Hmm." Grace sat back and took a bite of food.

"What? Is that strange?"

"Not strange, just different from how I grew up. My parents worked hard, but they thought that entitled them to keep what they had. I've heard my father complain many times about being 'hit up for charity'. I even heard him say once that people should make their own way, and if they couldn't afford it, then that was their problem."

"Even for a church or a hospital?"

Grace nodded. "His company was asked to sponsor a hospital benefit once, and he flat-out told them no."

"Wow. That's harsh. He didn't even want to do it for a tax donation?"

She shrugged. "I guess not. He's a principle kind of man, so if he doesn't want to give something away to someone, he won't, not even if he would benefit from it."

"I bet that was interesting to grow up with a dad like that."

Grace nodded slowly. "It was. He wasn't cruel, and he was kind to me and my sister, but it was always about what was right and fair. And what was best for me to grow up into a responsible adult. Like he wouldn't spend more on my first car than he spent on my sister's, and they would calculate what they bought us for Christmas to the dollar to make it fair. I had to earn my own way through college or not go because it wouldn't be fair for him to give me a handout."

"You're his daughter. I wouldn't call that a handout."

"I know, but he would." Grace took a deep breath and blew it out then looked away as if she wanted to change the subject. "This food really is delicious. Everyone's right when they say your mom is the best cook."

"Yes, I know. It's a miracle I don't weigh four hundred pounds."

"That might have something to do with how hard you work every day," Grace said.

Colton chuckled. "Yes, I'm sure it does."

"I admire that," she said. "My dad works in an office

every day, and there's nothing wrong with that, but I'm impressed with the work you do all day." She cleared her throat. "All of you, I mean. I'm sure your brothers all work very hard."

"We do. And my mom too."

Grace smiled. "I can tell. I think I could eat off this for a week."

Colton laughed. "At our house, this wouldn't even feed us for one meal."

Grace laughed too. "Well, I have to say, this is the nicest meal I've had in a long time."

With the company at this picnic, Colton had to agree with her.

5

Grace leaned back at her desk. It was Tuesday afternoon, and she could sit twirling her thumbs if she wanted. She had already reorganized her desk, eaten lunch, and answered the two phone calls that came in. Pastor Judson had been in a counseling session for the last hour, so she just sat in the quiet. Maybe she should bring a book to read.

Not that she would complain. She didn't mind the quiet. She did wonder if it was wrong to take a salary for a job where she hardly worked some days. But then she remembered on Thursday she would be helping prepare curriculum for the children's ministry, and Friday she would be printing and copying the church bulletin, and with her fights with the copier, that could take her all day.

The sound of voices coming down the hall caused her to jump. She leaned over and pretended to be studying the computer screen.

"Grace," Pastor Judson said, "can you put Mr. and Mrs.

Lane on my calendar for next Wednesday? I don't think I have anything that afternoon."

Grace reached in the drawer for the paper calendar. She had mentioned to Pastor that she could set up a digital calendar, but he only smiled and said he liked doing it the old-fashioned way.

She flipped a few pages and found the day. "Your afternoon is open. What time?"

"Is two o'clock still good?" Pastor Judson asked the couple.

Grace watched the woman nod.

"I'll put it down." Grace looked away as Pastor Judson walked the couple out. She never knew what to say to people after an appointment with the pastor. Saying, "Have a great day," or "see you next week," just felt trite for people who were going through a hard time.

When Pastor Judson came back, he looked stressed. "That was a long session." He never discussed his appointments, but he looked like he had taken on their burdens himself. He sighed. "Now, I've heard that there's a faucet dripping in the bathroom near the sanctuary. And a leak in the roof in the fellowship hall."

Grace felt terrible for him. "Isn't there someone who could help you with that? It seems like a lot for one person."

Pastor Judson rubbed the back of his head. "It is. I don't mind, but honestly, this isn't my area of expertise. We've talked about having a maintenance person for a long time, but I've never taken the time to find someone for the job."

"It wouldn't be a full-time job really. And maybe someone would even volunteer. Maybe one day a week to come in and check on things. We could keep a list, as long as nothing is an emergency, and then they could complete all the tasks at one time."

Pastor Judson brightened at the suggestion. "That is a wonderful idea. And I think I know just the right person, if he'll agree to it."

Grace smiled. "I'm glad I could help."

Pastor Judson moved toward his office, seeming a little lighter than before.

Grace's heart felt lighter too, knowing she had been helpful. It was a new experience to have one of her ideas be called wonderful. She had long since stopped making suggestions in her family or to Blaine. Her ideas and thoughts were unwelcome to them.

Later that afternoon, she looked up when the office door opened. She prepared her smile and a welcome greeting but stopped when she saw the man step in the door. Her heart skipped a beat at the sight of him. "Colton," she said, unable to hide the pleasure in her voice.

"Hey," he said, removing his cowboy hat. "Pastor Judson asked me to stop by."

"Oh," Grace said, realizing why he had been asked to come. Why did that excite her that he might be spending more time around the church? It wasn't to see her. He would never be interested in a real date with her. She would only hold on to the picnic memory as a fun time with a wonderful man. "He's back in his office. I can get him."

"No need," Pastor Judson said, entering the room. "Colton, thanks for coming. I won't beat around the bush. Grace had a wonderful idea for us to have a part-time handyman for the church. It would only be about once a week, maybe even every other week. Grace will be keeping a list of jobs that need to be done, so unless it's something that has to be handled right away, it wouldn't be too demanding. I know you're busy with work on the ranch, but I wondered if you might be willing to take on the job."

Colton's forehead creased as if he were considering it, but then quickly said, "Yes, of course. I would be happy to."

"Excellent! You don't have to start right away, but there are a few things on our list."

"Sure, I've got my tools in my truck. Since I'm here, I might as well tackle a few things. Hawk and Lawson can handle the ranch this afternoon."

"All right then. I'll show you what we need." Pastor Judson led the way down the hall. "Colton, you don't know what an answer to prayer this is."

Colton turned and flashed a smile at Grace. "For you and me both."

COLTON TIGHTENED THE BOLT ON THE PIPE AND ROSE FROM the floor. "That should do it," he said to no one. He crossed his arms and looked at the job, pleased at the work he had done. Pastor was right, he was busy at the ranch, but he was the first person Pastor Judson had thought of, and that meant a lot to him. He didn't ask any of his brothers. Only Colton. Besides, his brothers seemed to think they could get along on the ranch without him, so let them do it one afternoon a week. If Colton could serve the church in that way, it would be worth it. And he certainly didn't mind that he would see more of Grace.

He had enjoyed himself more than he could have imagined at their picnic. When he'd asked her to bid on his basket, he had hoped to avoid an awkward interaction with a woman who might be chasing after him. Instead, he had a lovely meal with a woman who held his interest like no one he had met. She was still a mystery to him, and his thoughts were constantly turned toward her and wanting to know her better.

Would she want to know him better too? If her smile when she saw him earlier was any indication, then he thought she would.

What if he asked her out for a real date?

Colton shook his head and began to gather his tools. Where did that come from? He wasn't a man who just asked a woman on a date. Especially one he barely knew. But what was it that Katie had said? *That's how you get to know someone.* Maybe that was true. Both of his married brothers had gotten lucky. Their wives showed up to the ranch and fell for them. But he knew it wasn't like that for everyone. If he did ask Grace out, where would they go? Shelby Springs only had the diner in town, and anywhere else would be a drive. Katie could probably give him a suggestion. Wasn't that what older sisters were for?

But no, why was he even thinking this? Grace moved to town for a change. Maybe she didn't want to jump into a relationship when she just got here. No, he would just be her friend for now. Certainly, she needed one of those.

He picked up his toolbox and started down the hallway. A door opened, almost hitting him in the face. "Woah."

"Oh, I'm sorry," Grace said, appearing from the other side.

He grinned. "No worries." He could feel his heart pounding and didn't know if it was from the near miss of getting slammed in the face or the sight of the woman who was consuming his thoughts.

"How did it go?"

Colton furrowed his eyebrows. Was she reading his thoughts? "What?"

"The repairs."

"Oh right." Looking at her, he had literally forgotten what he had just been doing. He really was in trouble. "Yep, it's all done."

"Thank you. Pastor Judson just seemed overwhelmed by the amount of work. I know it's a big relief to him for you to take over."

"I'm happy to help. I don't know everything, but I can do a lot, and if I don't know how, I can learn."

"I believe it. You seem like the kind of man who gets the job done."

His chest swelled as he looked at her. "I do my best. But it's nice for someone to notice."

"I notice you."

Colton's eyes snapped to hers. The kindness and sincerity there pushed him, and before he could stop himself, he blurted out, "Would you like to go to dinner with me?"

Grace's eyes grew wide. "Tonight?" she asked, her voice sounding shocked.

"No, not tonight. I mean, it doesn't have to be tonight. I didn't mean, um, anytime really. Well, anytime you're free and I don't have to sleep with the cows."

Grace giggled as he tripped over his words. "Is that something you do a lot?"

Colton rubbed the back of his head. "Well, sometimes. Not that often. I just mean if you're free and I can get away from the ranch." He cleared his throat. "Would you like to go to dinner with me?"

Grace blinked, and her eyelashes seemed to go on for miles. She looked up at him. "I would like that a lot."

Colton sucked in a breath. "Okay," was all he managed to say.

"Okay," she repeated after him.

"Friday?" he asked.

Grace nodded.

"Okay," he said again. "See you then." He turned and walked down the hall and out the door before he could make more of a fool of himself. Once he was in his truck with the door closed, he remembered he was supposed to go tell Pastor Judson when he was done. He had completely lost track of what he was doing. He ran his hand over his face. How could he go back in and see her? He could just leave and call Pastor to let him know he was gone. No, he was a man. He would face up to it.

He climbed back out and walked toward the church. Before he reached the door, Pastor Judson walked out, and Colton breathed a sigh of relief.

"Hey, Pastor, I was just coming to tell you I'm all finished."

"Grace told me you were leaving. At least I think that's what she said. She looked a little in a daze. You wouldn't know anything about that would you?"

Colton grinned. "Maybe, maybe not." He turned to go.

"I'll see you Sunday, Pastor, and I'll be back next week to do whatever is on the list."

He thought he heard Pastor Judson chuckle as he climbed into his truck. One thing was for certain. He didn't think he could be just friends with Grace for very long.

6

Grace stared at the message on the screen. She had stayed away from her social media accounts, and her phone was on the table at her parents' house. But she had logged in on the church computer. Surely, that would be all right. That was what she thought, until she saw the message from Blaine.

She swallowed hard as she skimmed it again. *You can't run away from me. It's time to come home and get on with our future. Call me and I will come and get you. We're meant to be together, and this whole charade is ridiculous. Come back, and by next spring, you'll be my wife, and we can forget this whole thing ever happened.*

Grace shivered just imagining his tone of voice if he were saying this. She knew without a shadow of a doubt that if he knew where she was he would have already been there. No, she couldn't let him know. And that meant hiding from her parents too. At least until he found someone else. As long as he still wanted to be with her, she couldn't let him know. Surely, he wouldn't find a place like Shelby Springs. He had been controlling, but he'd never been physical with her. She had a feeling if he found her now that might change.

Signing out of the social media site, she let out a sigh. Could she stay in Shelby Springs without anyone finding out her secret and without Blaine finding her? Grace whispered a prayer that she could. Even as she did, she knew that keeping a low profile and not getting too attached was the only way to do it.

Colton.

It would be a disappointment, but she couldn't go to dinner with him. What was she thinking when she said yes? Eating the picnic lunch with him was one thing; he had asked her to help him out by bidding. And she had loved every minute of their lunch and conversation. But it wasn't real. Going on a date with him would be a lie. And her life here had started with a lie, but she couldn't start a relationship on a false assumption.

Her eyes welled up with tears. No, Colton was a nice guy. Too nice of a guy for her to lie to him. She would have to let him down.

Closing down the computer, she pressed the button to switch the phones to go to the answering machine. She gathered her things and stood to go. Pastor Judson had already left; he needed to stop by and see a church member on his way home. Grace pulled out her keys and turned out the lights in the office. As she pulled the door shut and locked it, she thought about how much they trusted her. They had given her keys to the church and allowed her to be responsible for the building on her own.

A pit settled in her stomach, reminding her they had placed their trust in a lie.

Once she was in her car, before she could change her mind, she grabbed her phone and typed out a text. *Colton, I'm sorry, I won't be able to go to dinner with you. I'm not ready to start anything since I'm still getting settled here. I hope you understand.*

There, that was mostly true. Except she wouldn't ever be ready to start something with Colton, since she couldn't tell him the truth. She had let him believe she was someone she wasn't, and now she had to play the part, but it couldn't be with him.

She tossed the phone in the seat beside her and drove home. If you could call it home. The guest house was nice, but it was another reminder that she was taking a place that had been prepared for the other Grace.

"Hi, Grace," Mrs. Gibson called out from where she sat in the rocking chair on the front porch as Grace climbed out of the car.

Grace lifted a hand to wave.

"How was work today?" The woman's voice was so cheery, it made Grace feel even more sad that she didn't feel the same way.

"Fine, thank you for asking." She racked her brain to think of something to ask. She was learning that in Shelby Springs it was important to keep up with people and ask about their lives. Grace squinted one eye as she tried to remember their conversation from the day before. "Didn't your son have a job interview?"

"Son-in-law." Mrs. Gibson smiled.

"Right, the one in San Antonio."

"That's right. Yes, he did. My daughter called and said he thinks it went well, but he won't hear anything for another week at least."

"That waiting is hard."

"It can be. But they've left it in the Lord's hands now, and we pray for peace in the waiting. And even if things don't go like we hope, we trust that He has a plan that is better than what we wanted anyway."

Grace stared at the woman, blinking slowly. How did she have a faith like that?

Mrs. Gibson stood from her chair and moved toward Grace as if she could see the question in Grace's eyes from across the yard. When she got close enough to reach out and put her hand on Grace's arm, she spoke. "What's the matter, dear?"

Grace tried to paste on a smile, but it didn't reach her eyes. "Nothing. I'm just in awe of your faith and how you seem to take things in stride."

"Oh, but, my dear, you have the same faith I do. You know Jesus, right?"

Grace nodded, afraid if she spoke the tears would come.

"Then you have access to God. You can ask Him to increase your faith. All you have to do is walk with Him, read His word, and pray. He will do the rest." Mrs. Gibson squeezed Grace's hand and smiled. "Besides, you must have faith that God has a plan for you. You left what was familiar to come to a new place and start fresh. It's no accident that God sent you here. He will do a work."

Grace swallowed to push down the emotion and squeezed the woman's hand. "Thank you," she squeaked out. "I know you're right." Before Mrs. Gibson could say more, Grace hurried up the sidewalk to the guest house. With the door closed and no one else to hear her, she pressed her back to the door and slid to the floor as the tears slid down her cheeks.

"God," she prayed out loud, "this wasn't how things were supposed to go. I planned to stay in my hometown with my family, get married, have a family, all the normal things. But I couldn't stay there. I was afraid of what my life might become. But I didn't plan to find a town with all these wonderful people in it, only to start a new life based on a lie. I'm not the woman they thought was coming. I'm just someone who happened to have the same first name." She covered her face with her hands. "Oh, it's all such a mess."

A quiet whisper in her soul spread over her. *I can make beauty from a mess.*

Grace sniffed as she let the words take hold. "God, can you make something beautiful out of my life? I've only made a mess so far, but I'm ready to let You have control. Mrs. Gibson says it's not a mistake that I'm here and that You have a plan. God, if you have a plan and You want me to be here, then I'll follow You. I've believed in You before, but I give You my life. I don't know what You might do with it, but I want to trust You."

Grace felt like an elephant lifted from her chest, and she could take a full breath for the first time in weeks. Maybe even years. She laughed as she breathed in and out and the tears still rolled down her cheeks. The mix of sadness, relief, and...what was this feeling? Peace? Yes, that was it. She hadn't felt that in a long time.

"Okay, God. You've got my attention. I'm following You now, so You have to show me what to do."

Her stomach growled at that moment, and she laughed again. "I guess you're telling me I should eat some dinner."

She stood and wiped at her cheeks before moving to the kitchen.

As she reached for a frozen dinner, she thanked The Lord for bringing her here, and for whatever He had planned next.

olton removed his cowboy hat and dropped it on the passenger seat of his truck before climbing out and making his way into the church for Sunday morning service.

It had been four days since he'd gotten the text from Grace rejecting his dinner invitation, and he prepared himself to see her in church. He never responded to the message. What did you say to a woman who agreed to go out with you with her eyes shining in delight, and then canceled only a few hours later?

He couldn't make sense of it, except that maybe she was being honest. She was here for a fresh start, and she had admitted that she'd gotten out of a bad relationship. Maybe she was afraid of starting again. Or maybe she was trying to let him off easy because she met someone else she wanted to go out with instead. That would be par for the course for him. It could even be one of his older brothers. That would just take the cake.

"Good morning." He heard the voice and stopped in

his tracks. He wanted to turn with a smile and greet her, but he kept his face and voice even as he replied.

"Morning." He turned then and looked at Grace. She smiled at him as if she had a secret he would want to know.

"I'm glad I caught you. I wanted to apologize about the other night."

He shrugged. "It's fine. You don't have to explain."

She reached out to put her hand on his arm, and he felt like electricity ran through him. "But I do want to apologize. I had a message from home unexpectedly that afternoon, and it kind of set me off. I'm still not sure I should jump into anything serious, but maybe we could go to dinner as friends? I would enjoy talking and getting to know you better."

This was the last thing Colton had expected this morning. He wanted to be happy that she was at least agreeing to spend some time together, but the flip-flopping was enough to make him dizzy. "Um, well, thanks. Maybe you were right though. I'm pretty busy with the ranch, and now the church and everything. So maybe we should just forget about it."

Grace dropped her gaze for a moment, then looked back up at him. She gave him a kind smile. "Sure, I understand. I guess I'll see you around."

"Yeah." It sounded lame, and he knew it, but what else was there to say? He gave her a quick nod before moving away. He sat through Sunday school with a cup of hot coffee in his hands that he never drank. He tried to focus on the teaching, but it was no use.

When he walked into the sanctuary for worship, his parents stood at the entrance handing out bulletins and welcoming people, just as they did every third Sunday of the month.

"Good morning, son," Mom said, reaching out for a hug.

When Colton pulled away, he saw that look on her face. Her smile was practically wicked.

"I heard you were talking to Grace this morning."

'Yes, ma'am, I was."

"Mmhmm. And what did she have to say?"

He didn't dare tell his mother what had happened between them. Not only would she not understand, but she would try everything to fix the situation, and he couldn't have that. "Nothing really."

"You two seemed to get along very well at the picnic. Do you think you'll see more of her?"

He shrugged. "I see her around town, and now that I'm helping with the church building, I'll see her there sometimes."

Mom elbowed him. "You know that's not what I mean. Are you interested in her?"

Colton was grateful that she lowered her voice for the last part, but it still cut through him like a knife. Was he interested? He had been a few days ago. Then he couldn't get her off his mind. But now? Now he didn't know what to think. "Mom, let's just drop it for now. Please."

She held her hands up in surrender. "Okay, okay. But I just want to say she seems like a sweet girl, and you seemed happier after the picnic than I've seen you in a long time."

Colton squeezed his mother's arm before walking past her to get to their pew for the service. There was nothing else he could say to her. Especially since she was right.

But something had changed, and then changed again, and he wasn't up for the game.

He stood beside his brothers as the service started. He held the hymnal open and turned to the right pages as they sang, but he remained quiet.

When the service ended, he hoped to make it outside and to his truck without having to talk to too many people. He moved with purpose down the aisle and was almost to the door when a hand gripped his arm.

"Colton," his mother said as she stopped him.

He turned to see who she was talking with and came face to face with Grace again.

"Colton," Mom repeated now that she had his attention, "I've invited Grace over for lunch, and I wondered if you would stay and let her follow you to the ranch. I've got to get to the house and finish making lunch before the family gets there."

"Oh, but I don't want to intrude," Grace said, her eyes darting back and forth from Colton to Lydia.

"Nonsense, we have plenty, and we love having guests for Sunday dinner. Besides, we haven't gotten a chance to get to know you yet."

"Yes, but—"

Lydia interrupted her. "Do you have plans for lunch?"

"No, ma'am."

"Wonderful! Then we'll see you there. Just follow Colton. Now I've got to run. I'll see you there." With that she hurried off, leaving them alone. As alone as they could be in church with practically the whole town.

"I'm sorry," Grace said. "I didn't want to be rude."

Colton watched her eyes and knew she wasn't trying to hurt him. "It's all right. She's pretty hard to say no to.

Honestly, I don't think you were going to get out of that one. Once my nephew fell when we got home from church on Sunday and had to go to the ER for stitches, even he ate Sunday dinner before he left."

Grace covered her mouth with her hand as she giggled. "Really?"

Colton couldn't help but smile. "Yes, really. He was fine, but Mom wasn't going to send them away without being fed. She likes to make sure everyone is taken care of."

"That doesn't sound too bad."

"No, it really isn't."

"I'm sorry though. I didn't push my way in or ask to be invited. She came right over to me," Grace said.

"I know, you don't have to apologize. Do you want to follow me or ride with me, and I'll bring you back later?"

Grace's eyebrows shot up. "Really? You wouldn't mind?"

He shrugged. "Not really. I do have to see to the cattle this afternoon. It's my Sunday to do it. So it might be later, but I don't mind. If you want to get back after lunch, you could drive yourself."

Grace pressed her lips together as if she were considering her options. "I'll ride with you."

Colton nodded slowly. He hadn't expected that answer. He didn't know why. Pretty much everything Grace did was the opposite of what he expected. "Sounds good. Come on." He stepped back to allow her to move out of the pew. As they walked through the crowd of people visiting, he wondered what it would be like to put his hand to the small of her back and lead her out of the building. Or even better, to hold her hand in his and pull her close. Why he tortured himself with the idea, he didn't know.

In the truck, Colton fell silent. His mom was trying to push them together, he knew that. But she didn't know that it wasn't going to happen. Grace had turned him down, and he wasn't going to ask again.

"I don't want things to be awkward between us," Grace said. "I know it's my fault. But I hope we can get along."

"Sure. We live in a small town, after all, we're going to be around each other," Colton said.

"That's true." Grace took a deep breath and blew it out. "So tell me more about the ranch."

"You'll see it in just a minute. But it's been in our family for three generations."

"And it's mostly cattle?"

Colton nodded, keeping his eyes on the road. "We have cattle and horses. And we have the horse training facility now. Sierra trains horses and gives riding lessons."

"That sounds fun. I've never ridden a horse before," Grace said.

"Really?"

"Really. I didn't grow up on a ranch."

"Right. I forgot you're a city girl."

"I think I'm getting used to it here though. Life is different, but the atmosphere is nice. It feels calmer somehow, and peaceful."

Colton stole a glance at her. Something about her seemed different. "I'm glad you like it. I honestly can't imagine living anywhere else."

"I never imagined I would leave my home either," Grace said.

Colton cleared his throat and asked the question that

had been burning inside him since the day she arrived. "So why did you?"

Grace looked out the window, and for a moment it seemed like she wasn't going to answer. Then she turned and faced him. "I had to get out."

His heart flipped inside him at the thought that she might have been in danger. "What happened?"

She bit her lip and blinked rapidly. "My boyfriend, he was trying to take over my life. He'd run off my friends and only wanted me to spend time with him. I tried to break up with him more than once, but he would act like nothing happened. My parents loved him. In fact, we met because he worked for my dad. So when I told my parents, they thought I was being ridiculous. My mom told me not to mess things up with him, and my dad already practically considered him his son."

"What do you mean he tried to take over your life?" Colton narrowed his eyes as he drove.

"He controlled everything. My schedule, where we went, what restaurant we ate at. He would tell me to change clothes if he didn't like my outfit." Grace put her hands over her face. "I felt like a puppet. And as sad as that sounds, I think that's what he wanted."

"That's awful. Grace, no man should treat a woman like that."

She looked at him and nodded as she took a breath. "I know. I'm lucky I do though. That happens to women, and they think there's nothing wrong with it until it's too late. But I knew better. Since my parents didn't believe me, I knew the only way to get out was to leave."

Colton swallowed to push down the anger rising in his chest. "That was really brave."

"I don't know about that. I just did what I had to do."

Colton had turned into the driveway, and he stopped and put the truck in park to turn and face her. "Grace, it was brave. You're right, you could have been stuck in that relationship forever, and plenty of women would have just suffered through it. But you did the right thing."

"Do you really think so?" Grace's voice squeaked with emotion.

"One hundred percent."

She breathed a sigh of relief. "Thank you. You don't know how much it helps me to hear that. I haven't told anyone that since I got here. No one back home would tell me this was the right thing, and no one else knows. Knowing you think it was right gives me so much comfort."

Colton couldn't resist. He reached for her hand and took it in his. "Don't ever doubt that getting yourself out of a bad situation was the right thing to do. God didn't want you there, and if leaving was the only way to be safe, then that is the right thing. And coming here to Shelby Springs was the right thing too."

"People keep telling me that God had a purpose for me to be here, so I'm trying to follow Him and trust His plan."

"I agree. And I'm sorry you went through that, but I'm glad that you're here now." He looked down at their hands together and held on for one more second before pulling back. "If there's anything I can do to help, I'm here."

Grace smiled. "You've helped me so much already. I don't know what I would have done that day if you hadn't stopped to help with my car."

Colton looked at her, allowing himself to take her in for a moment. "I'm glad I could help. But knowing what you've been through, I'm sure you would have figured it out. You're stronger than you think."

"I hope so. I've spent a long time being treated like a child and told what to do." Grace sniffed.

"Take it from me, just because you're treated like a child doesn't mean you aren't capable. You can do anything you put your mind to."

"Thank you. That's a good thing too, because I'm not sure I'm ready to walk into that house full of people I don't know, especially when you're all part of such a wonderful family."

"One thing about coming to Sunday dinner at the Macklin's house: once you walk in that door, you're part of the family."

"Well then, what are we waiting for?"

Colton considered not telling her the truth, but after their conversation, he knew he had to be honest. "I guess I just wanted to keep you to myself a little bit longer."

Grace's cheeks flushed pink. "I can't say that I mind that either."

"Maybe we can make more time for that."

Grace smiled, sending his heart racing. "I sure would like that."

8

*G*race had enjoyed church immensely that morning. She had been to church so infrequently the last few years that she couldn't remember the last time she had been back home. Maybe it was Christmas? But the church was formal and stiff and she'd spent the whole time worrying if she was standing up or closing her eyes at the right time and if she would disappoint Blaine.

But today was different. She felt so welcomed by the people here. They accepted her better than her family who had known her all these years. And now she felt the peace that God was pleased with her, and she could rest in His presence as she sat in the church service.

But she hadn't expected Mrs. Macklin to invite her to their home. She whispered a prayer that God would take away her anxiety, but years of worrying what everyone thought of her had dug itself deep into her mind. Would the Macklins like her? Would they grill her with questions about her past and why she was here? And still she had to worry that they would discover she hadn't told the truth when they thought she was the other Grace.

She took a deep breath as she walked up the porch steps and through the door that Colton held open. She reminded herself that this wasn't her parents' house; it was a real, loving and kind family, and they wanted to know her.

She stopped just inside the door, and Colton stepped close behind her. Shivers ran down her spine when he leaned down and whispered, "It will be fine. They don't bite."

He stepped in front of her to lead the way. "And I'll sit by you."

Grace felt her cheeks flush as she smiled. "Deal." What a different kind of man he was. He wasn't making a demand, but an offer, and it gave her the confidence to walk in the room.

The foyer opened up to the large kitchen and dining room, and the house rumbled with the noise of the entire family gathered around.

"Welcome!" Lydia called out. "I'm so glad you came. Have you met everyone?"

"Um." Grace looked around the room. "Some of them, but not everyone." And to be honest, she didn't remember any of their names.

"Come on." Lydia looped her arm through Grace's. "These are my daughters-in-law, Katie and Sierra."

Grace nodded and smiled at the women.

"It's nice to meet you," Sierra said.

"Yes, we're always glad to have more girls around. We're still sadly outnumbered," Katie said.

"But maybe we'll add another girl with this little one." Lydia patted Katie's round stomach.

"Maybe, maybe not." Katie shrugged.

"You're not finding out the gender?" Grace asked.

Katie shook her head. "We thought it would be fun to wait." She grimaced. "Honestly, now I feel like maybe that was a mistake. I'm dying to decorate the nursery. But Sawyer is sticking to his guns."

Sierra laughed. "Jenson says if we have a baby, we will find out for sure. He had a big enough surprise with Naomi and Benji."

"Your kids?" Grace asked, trying to keep up with all the names.

"Yes, they're ours, but they're Jenson's niece and nephew. He didn't know about them until the day before they came here."

"Wow. Yep, that would be enough of a surprise for a lifetime," Grace said.

"They went home with a friend after church. You'll have to meet them another time," Sierra said.

"You girls can chat at lunch. Come on, Grace," Lydia said as she made her way around the room. "This is my husband, James. Have you met Grace yet? You know she's the new secretary at the church."

"Yes, yes." He reached out to take her hand. "We met your first Sunday, but I'm sure you met a lot of people that day. We're happy to have you here."

Grace nodded. "Thank you."

"And these are all the boys." Lydia pointed as she listed them. "Sawyer, Jenson, Titus, Lawson, Hawk, Garrett, and you know Colton."

"Oh you do?" Jenson asked, exaggerating each word.

Grace felt all eyes on her. "Well, yes, we met the day I arrived in town. He saved me, actually. I was stranded on the side of the road."

"Oh yeah," Hawk spoke up. "We heard that story from Colton, but we were sure he made it up."

"I can assure you it's true. He took care of my car and everything. I don't know what I would have done if he hadn't shown up," Grace said.

"Well, that was very helpful of you, son," Lydia said. "Although, I certainly believed you when you told us."

"Who's ready for food?" Colton asked, clearly hoping to change the subject.

"Oh, yes, we're all ready," Lydia said.

"Then we'll pray so we can eat," Mr. Macklin said, reaching for his wife's hand.

Grace watched as the other men bowed their heads, and Sawyer and Jenson moved to stand with their wives.

Grace closed her eyes and bowed her head.

Mr. Macklin began, "Dear Heavenly Father, thank You for Your Sabbath. Thank You for the service at church this morning where we heard Your word, and for this time together with our family. Bless this food that You have provided. Thank You for everything You've given us. Be with us now as we share in this time together. Amen."

The family echoed "amen" around the room. Sierra moved forward and took Grace's arm. "Come with us. Ladies eat first."

"Oh, that's polite of them," Grace said.

Sierra laughed. "Maybe, but I think it's because if they went first, there wouldn't be anything left."

Grace laughed too. "I bet. I can't imagine cooking for all of them."

"Lydia is a saint and a genius cook," Katie said. "She's been teaching me for a while now, and I can do it. But I'm just copying her and making recipes that she's made a hundred times. She's the one who figured it all out."

"Do you like to cook?" Sierra asked.

"Me?" Grace was surprised at the question. "I like the idea of cooking. But I haven't done it much." She would hate to admit that this was the first home-cooked meal she'd had since she arrived here.

"If you want to learn, there's no one better than Lydia."

"Oh I would love to teach you," Lydia said. "If you're interested."

"I am, really," Grace surprised herself by saying. "I can make scrambled eggs, and I've made a cake from a boxed mix once, but that's about it."

"What are your hours at the church office?" Lydia asked.

"I go in at nine, and most days I leave by three. Sometimes, I stay longer if Pastor Judson has an appointment."

"That's perfect. If you want to come by any day after you get off work, I usually start preparing dinner around four or four-thirty."

"Really? You wouldn't mind?" Grace's eyes were wide.

"Not at all! I would love to teach you, and it would be a help to me to have an extra hand in the kitchen."

"If you're sure, I really would like to try."

"Yes, I'm sure. You just tell me what day, or honestly just show up. I'm here every day."

Grace pondered the kind of dedication it took to take care of a family day in and day out. Would she have what it took to do that? All she'd ever been expected to do was be a good business wife. Her mother had taken care of their family, but it was different. Grace didn't think it took as much dedication to hire a maid and order in food.

"Thank you, Mrs. Macklin. I'll be here."

She didn't want to insert herself into the family, but if Lydia said it would be a help, then maybe that was something she could do.

The other women chatted about their plans for the week, and Grace went through the line, dishing out a serving of a delicious smelling chicken entree and a salad. The oven timer beeped, and Lydia went to take out a giant pan of brownies. Grace's mouth watered as she moved to the table. For a moment, she was uncertain. Did they have special places where everyone sat?

Sierra sat on one side of the table and pointed to a spot for Grace. "Have a seat. The boys can sit wherever." She grinned. "But Colton usually sits on that end."

Grace looked away and didn't respond. Still, she was grateful to know.

After the men loaded their plates, they came to join the women at the table. Sawyer and Jenson sat next to their wives, and Colton took the seat next to Grace, as promised.

"So, Grace, you're from Louisiana, is that right?" Katie asked.

"That's right. I've lived there my whole life."

"But you like Texas better, now, right?" Jenson asked.

Grace grinned. "Hard to say for sure, since I've only been here a few weeks, but yes, so far, Texas is much better."

"Did you work at a church there too?" Katie continued.

"Oh, no, this is my first time working at a church. But I did some office work for my father's company."

"That's nice. What kind of work does he do?"

Grace swallowed hard, hoping this was the last question about her parents. "He runs an investment company."

"What did your parents think about you moving to Shelby Springs?" Lydia asked.

"Well, umm," Grace stammered as she looked to Colton next to her.

He cleared his throat. "I think that's enough grilling Grace for one meal."

"Sure, let's move on to someone else," Hawk said, scanning everyone at the table.

Colton spoke up loudly before anyone else could get a word in. "Yes, so, Lawson, how's your rodeo lessons coming along?"

Lawson's eyes darted back and forth. "I'm not taking rodeo lessons. I'm just helping Knox with his practice."

"And you're not going to try any of it yourself?"

Everyone looked at Lydia, who stared at her plate and threaded her fingers together.

"No, I'm not. I'm just helping out."

"Mmhmm." Colton gave him a knowing look.

"Katie's had an ultrasound this week," Sawyer spoke up.

"Oh, yes, I have pictures!" Katie said, standing up and hurrying out of the room.

Grace watched as she returned and everyone oohed and ahhed over the black-and-white images of the baby's face. What was it like to be part of a family where they supported each other, and grilled each other, as Colton had put it.

She wasn't convinced she would ever be part of this family, but just knowing that one like it existed gave her hope for her own future.

olton watched as Grace walked to her car and waved when she unlocked it and climbed in. The ride back to the church had been pleasant. Grace wasn't overly chatty, but that was fine with him.

She had waited patiently while he did ranch chores and even rode out to the pasture with him while he took care of the herd. This morning he had started out by telling her he wasn't interested in starting anything. Now he felt like they had already started down that road.

He had often thought about what he would look for in a wife. He would need someone who understood the demands of ranch life, and someone who could hold their own with his family. Today she had shown him she could do both.

Colton turned his truck back toward the ranch and picked up his phone to call his brother.

"Hey, Colt," Sawyer answered.

"Hey. I just wanted to ask how Katie was. She seemed pretty tired when y'all left the house."

"Yeah, she was. But she's fine. I've heard being tired is just part of it at this point."

"Yeah, I guess so."

"I appreciate you calling to check, but that's not all you called for, is it?" Sawyer asked.

Colton sighed. "No, not really."

"So you like her, huh?"

"Is it that obvious?"

Sawyer chuckled. "A few years ago, I would have been totally oblivious to it. But now I know what it looks like to fall for somebody. So yes, to me, it's obvious."

"It's so strange. I just met her, but I feel like I can talk to her. She's just comfortable and down-to-earth. I just like being around her."

"That's how it starts."

Colton took a deep breath and blew it out. "So what now?"

"You ask her out."

"Actually, I did."

"Tonight?"

"No, I asked her out last week. She said yes, and then she changed her mind, and then she changed it back. I don't know for sure, but I think she was scared because she had a bad relationship before she came here."

"Hmm. Then I would say you need to tread lightly and go slow. You don't want to scare her off, but you also don't want to let her slip away."

"Ugh, that sounds complicated."

"Trust me," Sawyer said. "With women, it's always complicated. But when you find the right one, it's all worth it."

"How do you know if you found the right one?"

"You're going to say this isn't helpful. It doesn't always happen right away, and I know it's trite to say, but it's just true. When you know, you know."

"You're right, that isn't helpful."

Sawyer laughed. "Listen, Colt, I've known you for a long time, and if you're interested enough to be calling me to have this conversation, I think you already know what you want."

MONDAY MORNING, GRACE LAY AWAKE IN HER BED BEFORE her alarm. She'd never been an early riser, but now she found herself staring out the window as the sun peeked through the curtain. One thought swirled around her brain: What would it be like to be the wife of a cowboy who was up and going this early?

She should push the thought deep down, she knew, but it wouldn't go away. Sunday had been such a wonderful day, and she wanted more days like that. She grinned as she remembered that she would be going to the ranch after work for her very first cooking lesson.

She sat up and stretched her arms over her head. If God woke her up this early, it must be for a reason. She wished she had a Bible to read, even though she didn't know where she would start or how to study it. Pastor Judson had a collection of Bible study books on the shelf in the office, and she planned to borrow one today.

Reaching for her phone, she realized she could open the Bible online, so she did a quick search for "read the Bible." One suggestion said to read one Psalm and Proverb chapter. That seemed like a good idea, so she clicked the link and read from the first Psalm she came to, Psalm 139.

"O Lord, you have searched me and known me! You know when I sit down and when I rise up; you discern my thoughts from afar. You search out my path and my lying down and are acquainted with all my ways. Even before a word is on my tongue, behold, O Lord, you know it altogether. You hem me in, behind and before, and lay your hand upon me. Such knowledge is too wonderful for me; it is high; I cannot attain it."

"God," she whispered, "do you really care about me that much? Me? I'm a nobody. I've never done anything worth anything. But I pray that You will use me. Make me who You want me to be. God, You are good. I know that much. Teach me how to do this walk with You."

Feeling lighter than air, she climbed out of bed. After a shower and a breakfast of scrambled eggs, she left for work.

She was very early, but there was nothing left to do at home. As she neared the church, she saw a number of cars in the parking lot. Was there an event she didn't know about? Pastor Judson hadn't said anything. Maybe she could sneak into her office and then ask him about it later.

Just as she reached for the office doorknob, a voice startled her.

"Grace!"

She turned to see Mrs. Gibson.

"Oh, good morning."

"Are you joining us for Bible study?"

"I was just heading into work. I didn't know about the Bible study."

"We're just starting our summer session, so this is the first time we've had it since you moved here. I'm sorry I didn't think to invite you."

Grace waved a hand in the air. "That's all right."

Mrs. Gibson glanced at her watch. "But you don't go to work this early do you?"

"No, I was just awake early, so I decided to come on in."

"Wonderful! God must have known you needed to be here today."

Grace smiled. "I guess so."

"Come on, we'll go together." Mrs. Gibson looped her arm through Grace's like they were old friends and led her to the front door of the church. A small group of women were gathered in the front in a circle of chairs. Mrs. Gibson walked right in and took a seat and pointed for Grace to sit next to her. "Good morning, ladies. You all know Grace?"

They nodded and greeted her.

"This is Mrs. Newell. She's leading our group this time."

"We're so glad you could join us," the woman said.

"Thank you. It was an accident, but I'm happy to be here."

Mrs. Newell smiled. "I don't think it was an accident at all."

Grace nodded. "I'm starting to understand that."

A few other women came in and took seats before Mrs. Newell called for everyone's attention. "I'm so grateful you're all here today. I've been looking forward to this study. In case you haven't heard, our study this semester is on the Sermon on the Mount. We'll be looking in Matthew, but you don't need any outside materials. I'll have a list of questions and some verses to read before next week, and you might want to bring a notebook to write anything you want to remember." She chuckled. "Unless you have a better memory than me."

Grace looked around and realized she was the youngest woman in the circle, probably by about twenty years. Before now, she never would have been excited about sitting in a group of women much older than her, but today she felt exhilarated. These were women who had lived life and who cared enough about Jesus to wake up early to come to Bible study. Yes, this was infinitely better than the group of friends her parents had pushed her to who could barely meet for coffee before ten a.m.

"Let's start with prayer." All the women bowed their heads as Mrs. Newell continued. "Dear Heavenly Father, thank You for bringing us together today. Thank You for each woman here with us. Whether they planned to be here or not, You had a plan for each of us. Bless the reading of Your word and use it to teach us and train us to be more like You. Amen."

"Amen," Grace whispered. For the next forty-five minutes, she listened as Mrs. Newell read the scripture and asked questions about what they read in the text and how it applied to their lives. She was overwhelmed listening to the women share how God had used partic-ular verses in different times in their lives. Finally, she blurted out, "How do you all know so much of the Bible from memory? I think I could quote maybe one verse."

Mrs. Newell gave her a kind smile. "The only way to learn it is to read the Bible often and commit the words to memory. When I was a young mom, I never thought I would find time to read the Bible every day, but when I memorized a verse, I had it with me all the time. So I started memorizing just one verse a week. When I got better at it, I started with two and then three until I memorized one every day. All those verses add up over time. I can't tell you how many verses I know by heart, but I can tell you they have sustained me in difficult times."

"I want to do that," Grace said, "but I don't know where to start."

"Why don't you start here, with the verse we read today. The beatitudes in Matthew 5 are wonderful verses to memorize. Start with one verse and build from there."

Grace nodded. "That sounds doable. I'll give that a try. Thank you."

"Of course. We're all here to help each other. I don't have it all figured out, but I'm happy to share what has worked for me, and I know these other ladies feel the same way."

"Thank you. I have to be honest, I thought I knew the Bible before I came here, but I'm realizing that I don't know as much as I thought, and I really want to learn."

"Of course, dear," Mrs. Gibson said. "We all still have a lot to learn."

"We're just about out of time, and I want to be respectful of everyone's schedules. What can we pray for you this week?" Mrs. Newell asked.

Grace listened as one woman asked for prayer for her son who was having surgery, and another whose husband was going through a hard time at work. Grace had never seen anyone open up so easily to a group. Her parents had taught her to keep family situations to herself. What would they think if she asked for prayer for them? Not that they would know, but she felt sure they would be horrified if they did. Grace's mind drifted to them and wondered what they were doing today and if they were looking for her. She hadn't left them any clue where she had gone. Maybe she could reach out to them after it had been long enough. But what was long enough? Would Blaine have to be engaged or married to someone else before she felt safe? And if that were the case, how could she let someone else be left in that situation? She needed wisdom, but she could hardly ask for prayer for that. So she kept it to herself and bowed her head as the women prayed.

Grace echoed the amen with the other women as they all stood. She glanced at her watch and realized it was time to get to work. She turned and said good-bye to Mrs. Gibson before making her way out the door and down the hallway.

"Grace, is that you?" Pastor Judson called from his office.

"Yes, it's me."

He appeared in her office. "I didn't hear the door, so I wasn't sure."

"Oh right, I came from the sanctuary. I went to the women's Bible study this morning."

"That's great. I'm glad to see you getting plugged in here."

Grace's heart soared, to her surprise. She did want to get plugged in here. She wanted to stay in Shelby Springs and be part of the community here. And just maybe she could get to know a certain cowboy better. Was it even possible? Would she be able to stay without anyone finding out she had let them believe a lie? And what about her parents and Blaine? Would they leave her alone here?

She shook off the negative thoughts and smiled at Pastor Judson. "It's really starting to feel like home."

"I'm glad to hear it. We don't want to lose you now."

"There's nowhere else I would rather be."

"Great," Pastor Judson said. "I'll be in my office if you need me."

Grace couldn't believe how true her words were. She said a silent prayer that by some miracle she could stay.

10

Thursday afternoon Colton climbed in his truck and tossed his cowboy hat in the seat. Sweat beaded on his forehead, and he wiped it with the back of his arm. He wished he could change clothes before heading into town, but he was already later than he planned. And maybe he was anxious to get to the church. He told himself it was to get started on the work, but he knew it was because of the person he wanted to see.

The drive to church felt longer than normal, and he found himself saying a prayer. "God, I don't know what You have planned here, but I pray that You will lead me in the right direction. We don't know each other that well, so help me to go slow and do things right."

When he pulled up in front of the church, he jumped out and was almost to the door before he remembered his tools. He smacked himself in the forehead. He was here to do a job, after all. He should actually look like he knew what he was doing.

Tools in hand, he walked to the door. The corners of

his mouth lifted as he gave thanks that Grace was responsible for keeping his list of tasks. Opening the door, his smile grew at the sight of her.

She looked up from the book she held in her hand and quickly set it aside.

"Afternoon," Colton said.

"Good afternoon." Grace smiled at him as if she were pleased to see him.

Colton hoped she was. "Good book?" he asked.

"Oh." She blushed. "Yes, it is. I didn't mean to get caught reading. I just had a lull and thought I would read a chapter."

Colton chuckled. "I'm sure it's fine. You're not working at a fortune five-hundred company. I'm sure you have some downtime."

Grace gave a laugh that sounded like relief. "It's true." She leaned over her desk and whispered, "Sometimes, I feel guilty that they pay me. The job isn't hard at all."

"But it's necessary. You've taken a burden off of Pastor that allows him to focus completely on ministering to the church. For him to stop and answer a phone call or print the bulletin took a lot of time and mental energy from serving the congregation. Now he knows you are here to handle those things, and it frees him up."

"Really? Did he say that?" Grace's eyes were wide.

"That's the reason we discussed hiring someone in the first place. And I know you've done your job well. I can see the relief on his face."

"That's nice to hear. I've never really been helpful before. I won't feel guilty anymore, now that you've told me that."

Colton's stomach twisted in joy and pain—joy that he

had encouraged her and pain that she felt she had never been helpful. "You're helpful here. And I heard you're coming out to help Mom with dinner tonight. She's so excited to have an extra hand."

Grace laughed. "I'm not sure she'll want my extra hands after tonight. I'm likely to mess things up, but I'll sure try."

"That's all anybody asks." He could stay there and talk to her all day, but there was work to be done. "Speaking of dinner, I should get to that list or I'll miss the amazing meal you're going to make."

"Oh, right." Grace looked as though she just remembered why he was here. Her eyes flashed with disappointment.

He desperately wanted to change that look. "If I'm done in time, you could ride with me to the ranch."

Grace smiled. "That sounds nice. But then my car would be here, and I would have to come back tonight."

Colton didn't hesitate. "I don't mind."

Her cheeks flushed pink. "If you're sure, I would like that a lot."

"Then I guess I better get to work."

"It's not a long list," Grace said, reaching into the drawer. She handed him the piece of paper.

Colton glanced at it and only saw two things on the list.

"They could have waited until next week. Pastor said it's fine if you come every other week, if there's nothing pressing."

"Yes," Colton said, "I know. But then I wouldn't get to see you."

Grace pressed her lips together as if she didn't know how to respond.

"Well, I'll get right to this, and then I'll be ready to drive you to the ranch."

"I'll be ready."

Colton reluctantly pulled his gaze away from her. His only consolation was knowing he could spend the evening with her when he was done.

He made quick work of fixing the doorknob that had fallen off in the fellowship hall. The broken handrail on the back steps took him a little longer, but he was happy to see it finished.

His stomach did a funny flip-flop as he walked back to the office. He'd only had that feeling a few times. And usually it was because of a horse or a job at the ranch. He was never more excited than to do his job well. But this was different. He couldn't get Grace off his mind. He liked thinking about her. He wanted to just be around her.

Colton walked in the office and saw her bent over her desk writing. He cleared his throat. "You ready to go?"

She rewarded him with a smile. "Sure am. You got it all done?"

He nodded. "It wasn't much."

"It's still helpful. You said I take a burden off of Pastor Judson, but you're doing the same thing."

"I'm happy to help. Come on, let's get going. Mom is looking forward to your visit."

Grace stood and gathered her things. When they walked out and she locked the door behind them, Colton walked to the truck and opened the passenger door for her.

Grace giggled. "Do you know you're the only person who has ever done that for me?"

"What? Opened your door?"

"Mmmhmm."

Colton closed the door and walked around to his side, his mind running as he did. "Are you serious? My mom would skin me alive if I didn't open the door for a lady. And that started when I was about six years old."

"That's a good thing to teach. But no, where I grew up, that wasn't something guys did. Or at least not in the circle we were in. It's safe to say that in my private school, everyone was out for themselves. Guys went after girls, but it was more about impressing them with their sports ability or their father's money than their etiquette."

"I'm not doing it to impress anyone. I do it because it's polite, and it's how men should treat a lady."

Grace turned to look out the window. "I'm glad you feel that way. My parents taught me it was most important to be independent and not expect others to take care of you. But I admit, doing things on my own without a community doesn't sound fun anymore. Here in Shelby Springs, people care about each other. I like that. I want to know and care about the people here, and I hope I'm someone they will care about too."

Colton's own voice shocked him with a tender tone. "I care about you."

That caused her to turn and look at him. Their eyes met for a brief moment, but something passed between them. Colton felt it like a shock to his system. Grace didn't speak, but he knew what she wanted to say.

Colton turned his attention to the road and focused on his breathing. Had he actually forgotten how to breathe?

In and out, in and out. What was it about this woman that had his head spinning in circles?

When they pulled up in front of the house, Colton felt disappointed that their time alone was over. Sure, it was great that his mom liked Grace too, and the rest of the family, but sharing her was harder than he thought. Couldn't they just turn the truck around and drive and talk without all of his brothers bringing up his less-than-perfect qualities? He took one look at Grace's smile as she looked at him before turning to open the door.

He sighed. She needed this too. She hadn't grown up with a family like his. Yes, his brothers drove him up the wall, but they cared about him. And his parents had encouraged him his whole life. Grace needed that in her life.

He only hoped she needed him too.

GRACE HAD NEVER BEEN ANYWHERE LIKE WHISPERING OAKS Ranch, and she'd never known anyone like the Macklin family. They welcomed everyone and made them feel like family. Her own family didn't even make her feel like family.

She walked up the front porch steps and felt like she was walking into the home she had never known.

At the same moment, her heart dropped to her stomach. Why would Colton want to be with her? She didn't have any of those things to offer. She didn't know what it was like to live in a real home with a loving family. How could he want to spend time with her? What would she do to make his life better?

She shook her head as she walked through the front door and moved into the hallway. They invited her to come, and she would enjoy it—for as long as it lasted.

She followed Colton through to the kitchen. Lydia Macklin stood at the counter but turned and brushed her hands off on her apron. "Grace! Hello, dear!"

Before Grace knew it, Lydia had moved forward and wrapped her in a hug. It took her several seconds to respond, then she closed her eyes and returned the embrace.

"I'm so glad you're here," Lydia said. "Colton, I'm sure you have something to do." She raised her eyebrows and tilted her head toward the door.

"Yes, ma'am, always have work to do." He gave Grace one last glance before he walked out of the room.

Lydia turned to Grace. "I've got everything set out if you're ready to jump in?"

"Yes, of course. Let me wash my hands." And with that Grace jumped right in. Lydia was a pro and made everything look easy as she chopped this and that and grated with a flip of her wrist. Grace was in awe.

Lydia would show her with a few instructions and then hand it off while she moved on to seemingly five other tasks at the same time.

"Where did you learn to cook like this?" Grace asked.

Lydia smiled. "I guess where most little girls learn. My mom and grandmother cooked all the time, and they brought me in the kitchen at an early age. I don't remember a time when I wasn't sitting at the counter helping make dinner or lunch every day."

Grace dropped her gaze to the counter. "That sounds nice."

"It was. It was a simpler time then, of course. My parents weren't rushing me out the door to play a sport or go to choir or any other number of activities. Oh I know all those things are nice, but I grew up in a time where we sat on the porch and watched the rain come in. Children were allowed time to be at home with their families. I played a lot, but I also learned the responsibilities of ranch life early on."

Grace swallowed to push down the emotion rising. "I bet it was a wonderful childhood."

"Yes, it was. No childhood is perfect, but I loved living here and growing up around the horses and the fields and our family."

"Do you ever get out on the horses now?"

"Sometimes, not too often, but Jenson takes care of my horse and makes sure she gets exercise when I can't get out to the barn."

"So what does a typical day look like for you?" Grace asked. Her own mother never stayed at home longer than a few hours during the day. What was it like to work in the home all the time?

"I'm up at least by five, earlier if I know the boys have an early-morning task. I make coffee and breakfast and have it out for them as soon as possible. Mr. Macklin still helps out around the ranch, although he's handed off a lot of his responsibilities now that we're getting on in years. It's nice to see him around the house more often. After the boys eat, I clean up the kitchen and make sure we have everything for lunch. Then I take care of the house. There's always laundry and cleaning to be done." She laughed. "Always."

"I'm sure. I can't imagine the amount of clothing that seven ranchers create."

"I'd be happy to show you exactly how much," Lydia teased. "But actually, I'm down to five."

"Oh, that's right. Does it lighten the load?"

Lydia sighed. "Not as much as you would think. But I'm happy with what I do. My husband and sons work hard outside, so I work hard inside. And I find ways to enjoy it. I play music through the house while I work. Katie even set me up with audio books, so I can listen through the day. But what really makes me happy is serving my family."

"I know they appreciate you. All I hear is how you're the best cook in town, probably the world."

Lydia smiled. "I'm glad they think that. I don't want awards for it. I just want to feed my family and have them enjoy it. Speaking of, let's teach you some more cooking skills."

Grace gave all of her attention as Lydia showed her how to dice onions and the technique for blanching vegetables before freezing them. She watched her face and saw the grin and the way she watched over the whole kitchen seemingly at once. Lydia really did enjoy her work. What would it be like to be a wife and mom? Especially of so many? Grace had never considered the idea of being a homemaker. But watching Lydia take such care and attention to her family made Grace want to spend her days in her own home.

And if it was the home of a cowboy, even better.

11

It had been two days since Grace had cooked and eaten dinner at his parents' house, and he hadn't seen or spoken to her since. He was shocked at how much that tortured him. All he thought about now was her. Her smile, her eyes, how she tucked her hair behind her ears when she was thinking about something.

He couldn't put this out of his mind. It was time to act on it. Before he could get more nervous, he picked up the phone, found her name, and pressed call.

"Hello," Grace answered. How did her voice always sound so cheerful and calm?

"Hey, it's Colton," he said, as if his number wasn't saved in her phone.

"Hi."

"Hi." For a moment, he forgot why he was calling. It was enough just to hear her voice. He cleared his throat. "Um, how are you?"

"I'm fine, thanks. You?"

"I'm good. At least, I think I am. Might be better in a minute though."

"Oh?" Her voice rose at the end in the adorable way it usually did.

"I have a question, and I'm hoping the answer is yes. If it is, I'll be much better."

"Well then, ask away."

"The county fair is coming to Madison. It's about thirty minutes away, but I thought I would go on Friday night, and I wondered if you would like to go with me."

There was a long pause on the other end of the phone. "So, if I don't say yes, you'll be worse than before?" She was teasing him, and it was enough to drive him crazy.

"Yes, definitely worse."

"Well, we can't have that can we?" Somehow, her accent was starting to sound more like Texas. "Sure, I mean, yes, Colton, I'll go."

His heart pounded at a speed he hadn't known possible. "Great. I think it will be fun."

"I'm sure it will. I've never been to a county fair before."

"You're kidding," Colton's voice rose in disbelief.

"Nope. Not once."

"Then you'll be in for a treat."

"I'm already looking forward to it."

"Me too," Colton said. He racked his brain for something else to say, but he was so excited she said yes that he couldn't think straight. "I guess I'll see you then."

"Sounds good," Grace said.

"Bye," Colton said. He thought he heard her giggle as he hung up. He must have sounded funny getting off the phone so quickly, but what else was there to say? She said yes, and that was all he needed.

***

GRACE STOOD IN FRONT OF THE TINY CLOSET IN THE rental house. "What am I supposed to wear to a county fair?" The small amount of clothes she'd brought in her suitcase was getting their share of use, but most of them were clothes she would wear to work or church. With Blaine scrutinizing her wardrobe, she didn't wear many casual clothes. She had a thought and grabbed her phone.

"Hello?"

"Hey, Katie, it's Grace."

"Oh, hey, how are you?" Katie sounded pleasantly surprised to hear from her.

"I'm fine, thanks. I was wondering, where do you go shopping for clothes around here?"

Katie let out a laugh. "That's something I spent a long time figuring out. If you want jeans and flannel shirts, you can find a few things at the feed and seed. But for anything else, I order online, or I drive over to Richland Mall."

"Gotcha. Jeans and flannel might be what I'm looking for." Grace laughed. "What do people wear to a county fair?"

"Are you going to the fair?" Katie's voice raised an octave.

Grace nodded, even though Katie couldn't see her. "It looks that way."

"Oh really? With who?"

"You don't think I'm going by myself?"

"Let's see, you're going to the county fair and you're wanting a new outfit to wear, so I'm guessing no, you're not." Katie giggled.

"You're right."

"So who's the lucky guy?"

"I think you can probably guess that too."

"Oh? Is it Colton?" Katie practically squealed.

"Yes, it is."

"I'm so glad! We've been hoping he would get it together and ask you out. Well then, in that case, I might need to take you shopping."

"Oh you don't have to do that," Grace said.

"I don't mind. Besides, I could definitely stand to get out of the house for a few hours. Sawyer is watching me like I might burst into flames at any moment."

"Don't you need to stay close to home so close to your due date?" Grace asked.

"I'll be fine. It's only forty-five minutes away, and anyway, it's closer to the hospital. If I go into labor, you can just drop me off." Katie laughed.

"Let's hope it doesn't come to that. But I could use a few new things, and if you think that's the best place to go, I'd love to go shopping." Grace knew she couldn't risk ordering anything online to be delivered here.

"Wonderful! Could you go today?"

"Sure. I have to work until noon, but then I can."

"Great! I'll come pick you up at the church. We can grab lunch and shop."

"Perfect, I'll see you then." Grace hung up, wondering what had just happened. Had she actually made a friend? A female friend who wanted to go shopping together. Her mother liked to call them, "Girls' Days," but those were more like her mother telling her what to pick out and what was wrong with the things Grace liked. Today, she could pick out whatever she wanted. Well, whatever her cash budget would allow.

Grace finished getting ready for work with a pep in her step and a smile on her face. She was going shopping with a friend and to the county fair with a handsome cowboy.

Work flew by with the anticipation of the afternoon. Right at twelve o'clock, Katie came into the church office.

"Hey." She flashed a smile that lit up her face before she collapsed into the chair in front of Grace's desk. She took a deep breath and blew it out, placing her hand on her round abdomen. "You ready to go?"

"I am. But are you sure about this?" Grace tried to keep her disappointment at bay as she looked at her new friend.

"Of course I am. Walking is supposed to be good for labor, but this heat is too much for me. I feel like if I'm outside for thirty seconds I have to sit down and catch my breath. But we can stay inside at the shops. I'll be fine." She stood. "Besides, it might be my last chance for a while. I don't think it will be today, but I have a feeling we'll have a baby before the end of the weekend."

Grace watched as Katie waddled toward the door. She thought about arguing, and then decided she'd better just try to keep up.

An hour later, the two women walked into the shopping center. Katie had barely touched her food from the drive thru, saying she was too full to eat much.

Once they were inside and Katie caught her breath,

she set to work. "All right, first things first, we need to find you the perfect outfit for your date."

"I didn't exactly say it was a date."

Katie gave her a look that said she knew better. "He asked you to go, didn't he?"

"Yes."

"And did he say, 'just as friends', or make it sound in any way like he wasn't interested in you as a woman?"

"Well, no."

"It's a date. And you know it."

"All right, he didn't call it a date, but I sure hope it is."

"Then like I said, let's find you an outfit." Katie set off on her mission.

Grace followed Katie around as she picked up different options.

"This dress would be adorable on you," Katie said, holding it up, "but you don't want to wear a dress to the fair." She shook her head. "I wish we could pick out something fancy, but honestly, what you need is a pair of shorts and a cute top."

"That sounds doable."

"Yes, I think so." Katie turned and headed to another section, Grace trailing behind her. "Look here." She started going through tops on a rack, making faces and quickly sliding them down the rack. "Oh here." She held up a light-green top with cap sleeves and ruffles that cascaded down.

"That's so cute. I don't know if it's really me."

"Oh?" Katie asked. "What type of clothes do you like to wear? What's a 'Grace' look?"

Grace tilted her head. What was a Grace look? Did she

even know? "I don't know. You know what, I'll try this on. Maybe it is me and I just don't know it yet."

"That's the spirit. Your style can be whatever you want it to be, but if you don't know, now's a great time to decide."

Grace nodded. "You're right. I've worn a lot of clothes the last few years that I didn't even pick out for myself. I think I've forgotten what I actually like. But this is cute. I love the color. Do you think Colton would like it?"

"On you?" Katie's eyes twinkled. "Absolutely."

"Let's find a few more things to try on. I didn't think flowy, pastel colored tops was me, but it seems right."

"You got it, girl."

In a short period of time, Grace had tried on a few pairs of casual shorts and six different tops. None of them were like anything Grace had worn in the last few years, and she loved them.

"This is so fun!" she found herself saying over and over. She had forgotten that clothes shopping could be exciting instead of dreadful. She could have shopped for the rest of the day but knew that her wallet and Katie couldn't handle it. "I think I'll get these two pairs of shorts and these four tops."

"All great choices," Katie said, stifling a yawn.

Grace smiled as she gathered her items and headed to the checkout counter. "This was fun, Katie. Thank you for doing this."

"I had a great time too. We should do it again sometime."

When they pulled back into the church parking lot, Grace climbed out with her bags in her hands. Katie got out and waddled around to give Grace a hug before saying good-bye.

As Grace climbed into her own car, tears filled her eyes. When she left the only home she'd ever known, she hadn't expected to find such a wonderful community of people. Now she had a friend, and she only hoped she could stay here forever with her new friends.

olton climbed out of his truck and shut the door as he turned to walk up the sidewalk to Grace's house. All day long he'd thought of nothing but her. His normal laser focus on the cows was interrupted by the memory of her smile and her laugh. What would it be like to walk around the carnival with her? Would people see them and give them those knowing glances that people gave to couples on their first date?

He took off his cowboy hat and held it in front of him as he knocked on the door.

Only a few seconds later, the door opened and Grace appeared. Colton sucked in a breath at the sight of her. She wore a pair of denim shorts and the light-green color of her shirt made her hair look even darker than normal and her eyes brighter.

"Hi," she said.

That one word was enough to make him want to pull her off the porch into his arms and never let go.

He cleared his throat and gripped his hat tighter. "Hi," he repeated. "You look really pretty."

"Thank you," she said, her cheeks turning pink. "You look nice too."

"You ready to go?"

"Mmhmm." She nodded.

He stepped back as she walked out and locked the door behind her, then led the way to the truck. He opened her door and took a deep breath as she brushed past him. Did she always wear that perfume? He hadn't noticed it before, but somehow she smelled like sunshine. It wasn't a heavy perfume like some women wore, one that smelled like you were hit in the face with a flower shop, but perfect for her.

He walked around and climbed into the driver's seat. "You smell nice too," he said. Was that something you were supposed to say to a woman?

"Thanks. I got a new perfume."

Colton smiled. "Oh good, I was afraid I had been oblivious to it before."

"No. I don't think you're oblivious at all."

"I hope not, especially when it comes to you."

Grace grinned. "So tell me more about what to expect at this carnival."

"I still can't believe you haven't been to one before. I feel like I should take you out to a nice dinner, but if you've never had it, you've got to experience carnival food."

"I don't need a fancy dinner. I would rather eat carnival food with you anyway."

Colton glanced at her out of the corner of his eye. "Remember that when you eat the food."

Her laugh echoed through the cab of the truck, and it caused his heart to thud against his ribs.

"I don't care, I'm ready for a new experience, and I'll take whatever you throw at me tonight."

The conversation never stopped on the drive, and the time flew until they pulled into the parking lot. Colton got out, and Grace jumped down before he could get to her door.

"Wow," she said as they walked toward the bright lights of the carnival. "There's a lot of people here."

"Sure are. More than I expected really."

He watched her eyes dart back and forth as if looking for danger.

"Don't worry," he said. "Stay close to me." He stepped toward her and slid his hand down her arm until his hand found hers. It sent a shiver up his arm to touch her, but holding her hand felt like coming home.

They walked on toward the gate where Colton bought their tickets, reluctantly releasing her hand. He took it again as they moved into the carnival. "What should we do first? Are you hungry?"

Grace shrugged. "A little, but is it a good idea to eat before we go on carnival rides?"

"Good point," Colton said. "What if we do a few rides, and then eat. If you even want to ride."

"Of course I do. This is my first carnival, and I fully intend to squeeze every ounce of fun out of it."

Colton squeezed her hand. "All right then, let's do it." The nearest ride was the tilt-a-whirl, and he steered her that way. The line wasn't long, but it was tight quarters. He didn't mind one bit standing close to Grace and talking and laughing as they waited. Grace watched in amazement as the cars spun and moved in a circle around the platform of the ride.

"Definitely didn't need to eat before we went on this thing," she said.

Colton laughed. "You're right." When it was their turn, they walked through the gate and found a car. Colton moved back to allow Grace to step inside the half-moon-shaped seat and then sat beside her as he pulled the bar down over their laps.

"This is going to be fun," Grace said, grinning from ear to ear.

Colton couldn't help but smile at her. She was like a little kid, experiencing it for the first time. "You better hold on."

Grace gripped the bar but didn't seem concerned about the ride. A loud beep sounded, letting them know the ride was starting. The car jerked to a start, and they moved in a circle as the car swayed back and forth. As they picked up speed, the car circled faster, and Grace's giggles grew. Colton's chest swelled as he laughed with her, the swaying and circling of the car pushing them closer and closer together.

By the time the ride stopped, they were out of breath from laughing as Colton helped her out and held onto her hand.

"Where to next?" Grace asked.

"I wasn't sure you would want to do more rides after that one, but you seemed to enjoy it."

"I loved it! Let's keep going."

"Another wild ride or something calmer next?"

Grace wiggled her eyebrows. "Wild."

"Wild it is." Colton tugged her toward the line for the

scrambler. They enjoyed that one as much as the first, but Colton was ready to slow down and talk. "How about the Ferris wheel next, unless you're afraid of heights."

Grace looked the slightest bit concerned. "I'm not afraid. Maybe a little cautious, but as long as you're with me, I'll be all right."

Colton wrapped an arm around her shoulders. "I'll be right next to you."

In a short matter of time, they were loaded onto a Ferris wheel seat and moving up into the air. Colton tucked her under his arm and reached for her hand.

"I think this is the longest amount of time I've seen you without your cowboy hat," Grace said.

"I didn't want to lose it on a ride."

"I like it. I can see your face better."

"Is that so?" Colton asked, holding his chin up in the air. "And you like seeing my face?"

"I sure do."

"I like seeing your face too." Colton grinned, but then his face turned serious. "Actually, I like everything about being around you. You're easy to talk to, and you light up the room when you talk. I want to be around you all the time, and I want to know everything about you."

Grace blinked rapidly as she looked away. He couldn't say for sure, but she looked a little frightened. When she turned back to face him, a smile replaced the look. "I want to know you too, Colton."

"Does it scare you?"

She pressed her lips together as if she were thinking about her answer. "It surprises me. I've never thought of myself as an interesting person. Easy to get along with, maybe, quiet, sometimes, but not the person that people want to sit and listen to."

"I'm sorry anyone made you feel that way. I think you're incredibly interesting, and I could sit and listen to you all day."

"You might change your mind about that. After a day, I'm pretty sure I wouldn't be interesting anymore."

Colton turned until his face was inches from hers. "I don't believe that. I mean it when I say I want to be around you all the time. Don't sell yourself short. I like you, Grace. I like you a lot."

His breath caught in his throat as he inched his lips closer to hers. He closed his eyes, and his heart threatened to pound right out of his chest.

The car jerked to a stop. "Everybody off," the operator boomed.

Colton's eyes flew open to see Grace had jumped back. Her face said she was disappointed to have missed that opportunity. She flashed a smile before she climbed off the ride.

"Come on, let's go get some of that delicious carnival food you've been talking about."

Colton laughed as he took her hand and followed.

He couldn't promise that the carnival food would be delicious, but he knew for certain it would taste better with Grace by his side.

13

Grace couldn't stop smiling. Not even if she wanted to, which she didn't. It had been that way ever since the carnival. Colton had been the perfect gentleman, opening her door, paying for her food, carefully watching out for her as they walked through the crowds. But more than that, it had been the most fun she'd had in a very long time. The only thing that would have made it better was if they actually got that kiss on the Ferris wheel. Oh well, she was sure there would be plenty of time for that. They didn't have to rush.

But the days dragged on when she didn't get to see him. He had been there Sunday at church, but he rushed out with a quick good-bye after the service. Something about grabbing a sandwich and moving cattle that afternoon.

Now it was Tuesday, and she sat at work, drumming her fingers on her desk. Pastor Judson was in his office counseling a newly engaged couple.

She practically jumped out of her chair when the

phone rang on her desk. She composed herself before answering. "Shelby Springs Community Church."

"Hey," said the voice on the other end. A voice she had come to recognize.

"Colton," she breathed his name. "Why didn't you call my cell phone?" Disappointment washed over her. "Unless, you're not actually calling for me."

"Oh, I'm definitely calling for you. I just didn't know if you answered your cell phone while you're at work."

Her smile returned. "Well that's true. You know we're very formal here in the office."

Colton chuckled. "So I've heard. I wanted to tell you we're having our annual barbecue at the ranch on Saturday. I hope you can come."

"Is it a big event?"

"Not really. It's a family thing."

Grace swallowed hard. "Family? And you want me to come?"

"Yes, I do," Colton said. His tone was confident.

"Well, if you're sure, and it's all right with your family, then I would love to."

"They'll be tickled for you to come."

"Then I wouldn't miss it," Grace said.

Colton rode his horse toward the barn. Sweat dripped down his cheek, and he wiped it with the back of his arm.

"Hot day, huh?" Jenson said as he rode up next to him.

"You got that right," Colton agreed.

"Looking forward to a break at the barbecue on Saturday?" Jenson asked.

"A break? Who's getting a break? I'll be up at the break of dawn cooking meat."

"Yeah, but it's different than working cattle."

"True. And yes, I am looking forward to it." Colton grinned.

"Does that mean that Grace is coming?" Jenson waggled his eyebrows as he tipped his cowboy hat back on his head.

Colton gave a quick nod. "Yes, she is."

"How's that going?"

"Good."

Jenson raised his eyebrows as if he were waiting for more. "Just good?"

Colton took a deep breath. "Actually, it's going great. We're still getting to know each other, but the more I get to know her, the more I like her. I really think that maybe I've found the one."

"The one? That's pretty serious," Jenson said, leaning over his saddle.

"I am serious. This could be the woman I want to spend the rest of my life with. She's kind and sweet, and she's fun and likes to try new things. I like everything about her."

"Then what are you waiting for?" Jenson threw out his arms.

"Nothing. I invited her Saturday."

"Bringing a girl to the family barbecue is a big step."

"I know, and I think a big step is what I need."

"I just want you to be sure."

"You don't even know her. Why are you giving me a hard time?"

Jenson pulled his horse to a stop. "Colt, I'm not trying to give you a hard time. I'm being serious. I know you like her, and I'm glad. I'm just saying now is the time to be serious and to really think about what you're doing."

Colton nodded. "That's what I'm doing. I'm ready for this to be serious."

"Great, then if you're sure, go for it," Jenson said.

Colton huffed. "I am, but I didn't need you to tell me. I can make that decision on my own."

"Well, anyway, I'm happy for you. I hope everything turns out just like you hope."

Colton watched as Jenson pulled ahead of him and made his way into the barn. Maybe he'd been too harsh. He was so used to his brothers treating him like the baby brother, he hadn't stopped to think maybe Jenson was just being a good friend. Maybe now that he was in a relationship, they would see him more as a grown-up. At least, he could hope.

***

SATURDAY MORNING, GRACE WAS UP WITH THE SUN. IT WAS too exciting to sleep in, even though she wasn't supposed to go to the Macklin's until ten or eleven. But everyone else would already be there, wouldn't they? That was because they lived there, but still. There would be work to do, and maybe she could help. She piddled around her small house, did a load of laundry, and washed the two dishes in the sink. As she dried them and put them away she thought about what it would be like to cook and take care of a home for a family as large as the Macklins. Was that what she wanted? She hadn't thought about it much in the past, but now it consumed her thoughts. Her parents expected her to be a good business wife and have the acceptable number of two children, both of whom would go to private school. But what if she wanted her own houseful of kids? And what would Colton want? They hadn't talked about any of those things. Her cheeks felt hot at the thought. Would he want to discuss those things with her?

Butterflies danced in her stomach as she realized she hoped he would. She wanted to talk about everything with him. Before she hadn't made plans for the future, she knew she would do what was expected of her, but now? Now she wanted to think about her plans for her life, and she wanted those plans to include Colton.

The smile stayed on her face as she showered and dressed, taking a little extra care with her hair and makeup, even though she would be outside sweating part of the day. By nine o'clock, she had wasted as much time as she could, so she locked the door behind her and climbed in her car.

The butterflies returned when she pulled into the driveway and the Macklins' house came into view. Would she ever lose the excitement of seeing him? She hoped not.

As she walked toward the porch, the screen door swung open. Colton greeted her with a grin that spread wide across his face. "Hey there, you're early."

She held up her hands and shrugged. "I just couldn't stay away any longer. I figured I could help in the kitchen."

"No chance," he said, surprising her by wrapping his arms around her and squeezing her tight. "You can come with me out to check on the meat."

Grace was disappointed when he released her. "Is that a two-person job?"

Colton smiled. "Does it matter?"

"No. I'm happy to go with you."

"Great, because I have something I want to talk to you about." Colton took her hand in his as he started walking around the house to the backyard.

"What is it?"

"Let's wait till we can sit down. I want to give you my full attention."

Grace's heart pounded at double speed. She had to remind herself to breathe as they made their way around the back and then as she took a seat and waited impatiently as Colton checked the meat.

Finally, he closed the lid on the smoker and came over to take a seat next to her on the patio furniture. He took both of her hands in his as he spoke. "I've really enjoyed the time we've spent together lately. I can't wait to talk to you every day, and I'm disappointed when it's time to leave. I don't know if you've guessed this, but being here today is a big deal for me. I've never invited a woman to our family barbecue before."

Grace giggled nervously. "I hope that's a good thing."

"It's a very good thing. But, Grace, I wanted you to be here today because you're important to me. I want you to get to know my family and be a part of my life. This is probably going to sound cheesy, but I don't want there to be any guessing. I want to know what we are. Grace, will you be my girlfriend?"

Grace felt as if her heart might burst out of her chest. Colton's face was so earnest and adorable. "I don't think it's cheesy," she said. "I think it's admirable for you to want to be clear. And I appreciate that you're telling me what you want, but asking me what I want. Right now, I want nothing more than to be in a relationship with you and spend time with you. Yes, of course, I'll be your girlfriend."

Colton let go of one hand to reach up and tip his cowboy hat back. He leaned in, closing the distance between them.

The back door opened, slamming into the wall. "Hey there, you two," Hawk said. "I thought I should check on the meat."

"That's my job," Colton said dryly.

"Well, it doesn't hurt to have two people check on it."

"I would beg to differ," Colton mumbled under his breath.

Grace squeezed his hand and gave him a smile. She knew now that there would be time for that later. "I'm going to see if there's anything I can help your mom with."

"I'm sure she would appreciate that," Colton said. "I'll be there in a bit."

"Perfect. I'll look forward to it."

Grace stood and held onto his hand, until the distance pulled them apart.

It felt different to leave him out on the porch this time. Sure, she would have rather sat next to him and ignored everyone else all day, but it wasn't the same disappointment now. They were officially together, and that meant they had plenty of time. She would enjoy the day with the whole family.

The screen door creaked as she opened it and walked inside. How wonderful to have a door that creaked in a home that was loved and lived in. She made her way through to the kitchen and found Lydia leaning over the counter. "Morning," she said.

"Hi, Grace! It's so nice to have you here. I was so thrilled when Colton said you were coming."

"Thank you for having me. I feel honored to have been invited."

Lydia came around the corner to give her a hug. "We're so happy. And I think it's safe to say we'll be happy to see you even more now."

Grace felt her cheeks flush as she grinned. "Yes, I think so."

"I'm so happy," Lydia said, giving her another squeeze.

"So what can I help with?" Grace asked.

"I'm just finishing up this pie to go in the oven. But I've got the recipe card out there for the vegetable casserole. Could you start on that?"

Grace nodded. "You know, a month ago, I would have said no way. I hardly knew how to read a recipe. But thanks to you, I think I can at least give it a try."

"I'm right here if you need me, but I have full confidence in you."

"I have full confidence in me too, but only because I've had a good teacher."

"We haven't talked much about your life in Louisiana. And I understand if you don't want to talk about it. I'm sure you left for a reason. But if you ever need someone to talk to, I hope you know that I'm here for you."

Grace's eyes glistened as she tried to focus on the recipe card. "Thank you. You don't know how much that means to me. I don't want to open that can of worms today. I would rather be happy. But I promise, we can talk about it soon."

Lydia patted her arm the way only a mother could. "No pressure, truly. Just wanted you to know I'm here."

Grace turned her attention to reading the list of ingredients. They worked side-by-side for the next little bit. Lydia pointed out where an item was in the kitchen and gave instructions as needed.

The front door opened and banged shut. "Hey, Mom, we're here."

Lydia practically squealed. "That's Sawyer. They're bringing the baby."

"Oh, I wondered."

"Have you seen him yet?"

Grace shook her head. "No, not yet."

"Come on then." Lydia brushed her hands off on the apron she wore and grabbed Grace's hand to lead her into the living room.

Sawyer looked like he had packed for a week-long vacation with the bag over his shoulder. Katie gingerly sat down on the couch with the baby in her arms.

"Hi there, little one," Lydia cooed.

"Hey, Mom," Sawyer said.

Lydia swatted his arm. "Not you. It's been a very long time since you were little."

Sawyer grinned as he took a seat next to his wife.

Lydia took the baby in her arms and sat in the rocking chair. "Grandmama is here, and I'm so happy to see you."

Grace stood in the doorway watching.

Katie motioned for her to join them. "Come see him, Grace."

Grace slowly made her way in the room and peeked over Lydia's shoulder.

"Do you want to hold him?" Katie asked. "When Grandmama has had her fill, that is."

Lydia laughed. "Well, that will be never, but I'm happy to let you hold him."

"Oh no." Grace held up her hands. "You hold him. I don't have much experience around babies."

"Neither do I." Katie laughed. "But you'd be surprised how easy it comes to you."

"Maybe later," Grace said. "He looks happy. I wouldn't want to disturb him."

"Mom has waited a long time for this," Sawyer said.

"Too long," Lydia said. "But I'm thrilled for it now. He's not my first grandchild, of course. I love Naomi and Benji to pieces. But he's my first grandbaby to hold at this age."

"What's his name?" Grace asked.

"Colton didn't tell you?" Sawyer asked.

"No, I don't think so."

Katie grinned. "They have plenty of other things to talk about."

"Oh, right. His name is Dillon James," Sawyer said.

"That's adorable," Grace said. What would it be like to be a married couple just starting a family? Is that what Colton would want? Her cheeks felt warm at the thought. "I should get back to the kitchen. Lydia, I think I can finish the casserole, so you stay there. I can holler if I need you."

"I'll join you," Katie said. "Dillon is in good hands, and I brought everything for the cheese biscuits, but I need to put them in the oven."

The two women headed for the kitchen as Lydia sat contentedly in the rocker.

"I never thought I'd live to see the day when Lydia Macklin would leave me alone in her kitchen," Katie said.

"She's smitten, isn't she?" Grace asked.

Katie nodded. "Mmhmm. I have to admit, I am too." She sighed a happy little sound. "And watching Sawyer with him is just a dream. I knew I loved him before, but seeing him as a dad just changes things."

"I'm sure he feels the same about seeing you become a mom," Grace said.

"I hope so. Some days I feel like I'm fumbling around figuring it out. I just want to be a good mom."

"I'm sure you will be. Just the fact that you worry about it means you're going to do the best you can."

Katie touched the corner of her eyelid as she sniffed. "I sure hope so. Sorry," she said. "It's the hormones. I just get emotional over everything these days."

Grace smiled and reached to touch her arm. "It's okay. I think babies are a good thing to be emotional about. And wanting to be a good mom is the most worthy goal I can think of." Her voice quivered as she got emotional too.

"Look at me blubbering when there's food to fix. Plus, I want to hear about you and Colton. I've missed out on everything since I had Dillon."

"It's only been a week." Grace pressed her lips together and dropped her gaze to the counter. "But, as a matter of fact, there is some news. No one else knows yet."

Katie squealed as quietly as possible. "I'm never the first to know anything."

"Colton asked me to officially be his girlfriend."

Katie's mouth dropped open. "He did? That's absolutely adorable. And I'm so excited! So it's for real now."

Grace nodded. "Looks that way."

"Well, of course, it was real anyway. You're at the family barbecue, so you're part of the family."

"People keep saying that. Is it really that serious?"

Katie gave her a serious look and nodded. "Oh, yes. Lawson was dating a girl last year, but he didn't bring her. He wasn't ready to commit. And now they're not together anymore. I'm not saying they broke up because he didn't invite her, but if he had been serious, she would have come. But Colton inviting you means he's sure about this."

"Wow. I had no idea. When he called, he said it was a big deal, but I didn't understand it was that big."

"Yep, it is. And this thing between the two of you is big."

Grace grinned. "I hope so."

"You hope so what?" Sawyer asked, coming up behind Katie and wrapping his arms around her.

"Never you mind," Katie said.

The back door swung open, and Grace listened as the boots thudded across the floor as she expectantly waited to see Colton walk in the door.

"Hey," he said when he appeared.

Katie giggled, and Grace felt her cheeks flush.

"What?" Colton said.

"Nothing. Katie and I were just talking while we finish up a few things."

Colton made his way over to Grace and slipped an arm around her waist. "Everything looks good in here. The meat should be ready in about thirty minutes."

"Then we better get a move on," Lydia said from the doorway where she stood with the baby.

The next few hours passed for Grace in a happy blur. The women worked together to complete the meal, then everyone worked together setting out the food outside as the men got the meat out. Grace thought it would be like every other day for the family with the meals they normally ate together, but the day was sacred.

Laughter rang around the table as the brothers gathered. They shared stories from their childhood and teased each other and encouraged each other.

Mr. Macklin cleared his throat when everyone had finished their dessert of peach cobbler and homemade vanilla ice cream. "It means so much to us that each of you are here. When we had our first family barbecue when you boys were kids, I'll be honest, it was because we couldn't go on a vacation that year. There was too much work to be done on the ranch, and not enough money to go somewhere, much less to pay someone to watch the ranch while we were gone. So we planned a special family day. Your mother planned the menu, and we had a water balloon fight. It was simple, but you all agreed it was the best day ever. Right then we decided to make it an annual event. We've added some family members, and we're thrilled about that. But we're mostly just glad that all of you still like being around each other and you want to come here for our special day to celebrate. We're thankful The Lord has blessed us with each of you."

Grace wiped at the tears in her eyes. She caught a glimpse of Katie across the table doing the same thing.

"This year we'd like to start a new tradition to go with the old one. Our newest grandchild is here with us today, and we would like to commemorate that. Naomi and Benji, this isn't your first barbecue, but since we're starting here, we want to include you in this.

"Sawyer and Katie, if you'll stand here with Dillon, and Jenson and Sierra, you and Naomi and Benji stand next to them."

The two couples and their children rose and stood where Mr. Macklin asked.

Lydia stood next to her husband, smiling, but blinking away tears. "Dillon, Naomi, and Benji, you're grandpa and I have chosen a Bible verse for each of you. This will be the verse that we commit to pray over you as you grow. We believe it's your parents' job to raise you, but we also believe you were born into a family of faith who loves you and will support you. We want to give you our family's blessing over your life."

Lydia paused to clear her throat and dab her cheek with a tissue. Then she held up a card as she read. "Naomi, our oldest granddaughter. We're so thankful for your life. We pray for you Matthew 22:37 'You shall love the Lord your God with all your heart and with all your soul and with all your mind.'

"Benji, our grandson, we pray that you will grow to be a mighty man of God. We pray for you Joshua 1:9. 'Have I not commanded you? Be strong and courageous. Do not be afraid; do not be discouraged, for the Lord your God will be with you wherever you go.'

"Dillion, precious baby, we pray for your Mom and Dad as they learn to be parents for the first time, and we pray this verse for your life. Colossians 1:9-10, 'And so, from the day we heard, we have not ceased to pray for you, asking that you may be filled with the knowledge of his will in all spiritual wisdom and understanding, so as to walk in a manner worthy of the Lord, fully pleasing to him: bearing fruit in every good work and increasing in the knowledge of God."

"Let's pray," Mr. Macklin said.

Grace was sure she heard some sniffles, even from the men.

"Dear Heavenly Father, thank You for our family. Thank You for the gift you have given us in allowing us to be parents to these men before us. Thank You for our grandchildren. We pray these verses over them and ask that You will draw them near to You. Open their hearts to the Gospel, and I pray that they will always love You God. Thank You for all You will do in their lives. Amen."

"Amen," everyone echoed.

Katie went to hug James and then Lydia with tears streaming down her face. "Thank you," she said. "I will never forget this."

Lydia hugged each of the children. "We hope you will never forget it either." She looked up at everyone else around the table. "Now, we've only got a year until the next barbecue, so who's going to be next?"

Grace's eyes grew wide as more than one person glanced her way. They looked away quickly as if they didn't want her to feel awkward, but it was too late.

"Isn't it time for Jenson and Sierra to have another one?" Hawk spoke up.

Naomi and Benji's mouths dropped open as they looked at Jenson and Sierra.

Sierra held her hands up. "No, no news in that department."

Grace thought she looked a little sad but didn't know her well enough to be sure.

"Well, we will be happy to celebrate with you all again next year, whether there are new babies or spouses or anything."

Colton caught Grace's eye that time, as he took her hand in his.

She didn't have to wonder if he liked her or if he was serious. She knew being here today said everything she needed to know.

Now she could only hope she could be here next year.

Colton laced his fingers through Grace's hand as they stepped off the front porch into the dark yard. "Today was wonderful," he said.

"Mmhmm," she agreed.

"But as much as I love my family, I'm happy to get a few minutes alone."

"Do you think anyone will come bursting out of the house to steal you away?"

"I'll punch them if they do."

Grace laughed. "I don't think you would."

"Nah, but I would want to."

"The family blessing at lunch today was very special," Grace said.

Colton nodded as they walked past her car, headed nowhere in particular. "It was."

"It was really a special day all around. All about family."

Colton stopped and turned to face her. "And how do you feel about that?"

Grace took a deep breath. "I love it. I know your brothers tease you, but I can tell you all care a lot about each other. And your parents just want what's best for all of you. I've never had anything like that before."

Colton stepped close and wrapped his arms around her. "This is your chance. You can have all of that. Grace, I'm trying not to move too fast, and I want you to have what you want, but I asked you here today because I've never met anyone else that I wanted to ask to come to the barbecue. I've never met anyone that I thought I could be serious about and that I wanted to be part of my life and my family."

Grace looked up at him, only inches from him now. "Do you really mean that?"

"Yes, I do."

"Colton, that's what I want. To be part of your life. I've never felt more at home than I feel with you."

"I feel the same way. You're a match for me in every way." He paused and gazed into her eyes. He could see the future there. "Grace," he whispered before lowering his head. When their lips met, it was as if fireworks exploded in his chest. He breathed her in as their lips moved together. Grace's arms went around his neck, and he pulled her closer, certain he could never get enough of her. Reluctantly, he eased his grip and pulled back as he kissed her jawline up to her forehead and then leaned back to look her in the eyes.

He studied her then. She didn't look scared or unsure. She looked confident and happy. He let himself press his lips to hers one more time before stepping back and taking both of her hands in his. "Grace," he said, "I want you. All of you, with me, forever."

Grace nodded. "That's all I want too."

"Let's keep walking. I'm not ready to send you home yet."

They fell in step beside each other. The quiet as they walked hand-in-hand was enough.

"I've never seen so many stars," Grace finally said. "I know that sounds silly, since there's the same number of stars in Louisiana as here, but at my parents' we have too many lights. Our house was in a neighborhood with a hundred other houses, and no one liked the dark."

"I know what you mean. Here there's nothing but sky."

"I like it that way," Grace said.

"So you don't think you would ever want to go back to Louisiana?"

Grace shook her head. "Definitely not. There's nothing there for me."

"Do your parents know where you are?"

She dropped her gaze and shook her head. "No. I didn't feel like it was safe for me to tell them yet."

"But you'll tell them eventually, right?"

Grace shrugged. "Sure. I mean, I don't hate them. I'm not trying to cut them out of my life forever. I just needed to get away, and if they knew where I was then…well, I wouldn't have been able to stay."

"I understand." Colton faced her and took both of her hands again. "I want you to feel safe. You can tell them when you're ready. But I hope if we make plans for the future, you'll be able to tell them."

Grace looked uncertain again but smiled as she stood on her tiptoes to kiss him. "I hope so too."

Grace paced the floor of her house. If it had been carpet, she would have worn tracks, but on the hardwood, she now knew every spot in the living room that creaked.

Colton hadn't said she should tell her parents right now, but she couldn't get the thought out of her mind. They didn't know where she was. Yes, she had needed to get away. But even if they weren't the most caring, supportive parents, they should know where she was now. Being around the Macklins had changed her way of thinking. She couldn't imagine if she had a daughter one day and didn't know where in the world she was for one minute. It would kill her. Even if her parents had wanted her to stay with Blaine, they must be worried about her.

But could she really tell them? They would surely try to convince her to come back and make things right with Blaine. But she didn't have to listen. She had no plans to go back. And now that she was building a life here, they needed to know that.

Her heart pounded so hard she placed a hand on the kitchen table and gasped for breath. "God," she prayed. "Help me. I wanted to run, but I don't want to keep this from them anymore. I have made my decision, and I'm sticking to it. They can't control me anymore."

The house felt silent and cold as she moved to her room and picked up her phone. "God, if you don't want me to tell them, don't let them answer," she prayed. She slowly typed her mom's number in and hit the call button. "One," she counted as it rang. "Two." Maybe she wouldn't answer. She could leave a voicemail. Maybe that would be safer. "Three." Her mom never answered numbers she didn't know.

After the fifth ring, her mom's voicemail picked up. Grace wasn't sure she even listened to her messages, but at least she could tell her she was all right. After the beep, Grace took a breath and launched in. "Hi, Mom, it's me, Grace. I'm sorry I left without telling you, but I just needed to get some space. I'm safe and happy. I'm in Texas, and I have a job and a place to stay. I just wanted you to know I was all right. I hope you and Dad are all right too. You can call me back on this number. I…" Grace stumbled over the words, but it was true, and she wanted to say it. "I love you, Mom. Bye."

When she pushed the button to end the call, she fell onto her bed and took in gulps of air. Maybe she wouldn't call back. Or maybe she would. Grace didn't know which would be worse, hearing her Mom's thoughts, or knowing she didn't care enough to find her.

After several minutes, Grace stood. "God, it's in Your hands now. I do love my parents, and I don't want to leave them out of my life forever. I pray that You would make a way for us to talk, and help them to understand why I did this. And if they don't, help me be strong and keep me safe. Amen."

***

Colton laced his fingers through Grace's as they strolled toward his piece of the property. "This is pretty much the only place we're guaranteed to be alone."

Grace laughed. "It does seem that way. Although I don't see any alarms or "No trespassing signs" so I'm guessing if they wanted to, they would just walk up here too."

"You're starting to catch on," he said. "But really, they won't bother us."

"So this is your place." Grace dropped his hand and walked forward, turning in a circle as she looked around. "It's nice."

"I used to come up here and walk around when I wanted to get away. That was before it was officially mine. Dad gave it to me on my eighteenth birthday, just like everyone else. But I had picked it out long before."

"It's nice to have a place to get away, isn't it?"

"You have no idea," Colton said.

"Well, I think I have some idea. I had to cross state lines to get away from my family, remember?"

Colton grimaced. "I'm sorry. I shouldn't have said that."

She held up her hand as he moved toward her. "No, it's all right. I know what you meant. And it's different anyway. I'm glad you could have some space up here." She looked away.

Colton stepped close. "What's wrong?"

"I called my mom today."

His eyes flew open wide. "Really? What did she say?"

Grace shook her head. "Nothing, she didn't answer. I left her a message and told her I was safe, and she could call me back on this number. But I haven't heard anything."

"Do you think she'll call?"

Grace shrugged. "No way to know, really. And I don't know what I want. If she doesn't call, it will hurt my feelings."

Colton reached for her and stroked her back as he held her. "I'm sure she's worried about you. Maybe she just needs some time to process it before she calls back."

Grace shrugged. "Maybe. I know she's probably mad. I left without telling them, and I left my phone behind and didn't tell them where I was going. I mean, I didn't even know where I was going."

Colton tilted his head and furrowed his eyebrows. "What do you mean? You didn't know you were coming to Shelby Springs?"

"Oh, I um, I mean, I didn't know when I started planning to leave."

"Did you go somewhere else before here? We knew you were coming for a few weeks before."

"No, I mean, it took that time for me to get everything together to leave," Grace said, clearing her throat. "Anyway, I don't know if she will call or not, but I did what I felt like I needed to do. If they're worried, I don't want them to be. I don't know that they will want to be involved in my life here, but at least they know where I am."

"Right."

"So what are your plans for the land here? Do you think you'll build a house?"

Colton nodded slowly, trying to bring himself back to the moment. Why did he feel so unsettled by her answer? He took her hand as they walked on. "I want to build it there, so there's space for a garage and probably a barn."

"You want your own barn?"

"Sure. I've shared with my brothers for a long time. I'll still work the ranch, but I want my own space for my home and for my horse. And for, well, whatever else comes along." He had been planning to say family, but he felt like he shouldn't say that to her just yet.

"I think it will be wonderful. Do you think you're ready to start the building process now?" Grace asked.

Colton looked at her and smiled. "I'm more ready now than I've ever been."

Grace flopped on her bed and put her hand to her forehead. "Why did I open my big mouth? I know he knew I was changing my story."

"God, I'm sorry, I should have told him the whole truth, but I panicked. What if he doesn't want to see me anymore if he finds out the truth? He's the only man I've ever felt this way about, and I just don't think I can stand to lose him."

Her phone beeped just then, signaling a text message. She glanced and immediately saw it was from Colton.

Hey, just making sure you got home safe. Are you coming to the ranch tomorrow for dinner?

She groaned. How could he be so nice to her when she had just let him down? She typed out a response. *Planning on it. Is that ok?*

Of course. Just wanted to know.

She waited for him to say more, but nothing else came.

Pulling herself up from the couch, she went to the freezer and pulled out a microwave meal. She didn't feel like pulling out what she had planned to cook for dinner. Colton had work to do at the ranch, so she didn't stay, and now cooking Lydia's chicken casserole dish for one person seemed a little ridiculous. She slammed the microwave shut and punched the buttons. Today was supposed to be a perfect day with him out at his land. Instead, she had a knot in her stomach for most of the time.

As she climbed into bed for the night, she checked her phone one last time. Colton had texted again. *See you at dinner tomorrow. I won't be by the church tomorrow, so come straight over when you get off work.*

Grace set the phone on her bedside table without responding. Why did his text rub her the wrong way? She was planning to go there when she got off, but she didn't need him to tell her that. What if she had other plans or errands she needed to run? She certainly didn't need him to start telling her when to be somewhere.

She sighed as she turned out the light and closed her eyes. It wasn't his fault, and she knew it. Just because she had messed up didn't mean she needed to create a reason to be mad at him. But it was easier to convince herself he was being pushy than it was to hope he would still care about her if he knew the truth.

The next day, Colton finished up his work as quickly as he could, although cows usually moved at their own slow pace, not caring that he had somewhere to be. Or rather someone to see. He told himself to push away the negative thoughts that Grace was hiding something from him. Why would she be? She had told him about her parents and her ex-boyfriend. What else could there be to keep from him?

No, she was just what she said she was. And she was the woman for him. Hadn't God brought her to town and stranded her on the side of the road just so Colton could be the first one to meet her? If God did that in his infinite plan, then who was Colton to sabotage it by thinking something was wrong?

Besides, she would be here tonight and they could talk more. He reached for his phone and pressed the button to call her. She picked up after several rings.

"Hey," she said.

Was it his imagination or did she sound agitated? "Hey, are you almost here?"

"Not quite. I had to stop at the store."

"Oh what store?"

"The feed and seed."

"Oh yeah. What did you need?"

"I just needed a few things. I'm on my way now."

"Okay. I'm just getting to the barn. But go on to the house and I'll be there soon."

Grace let out a forceful breath. "Okay."

"See you in a little bit," Colton said, lowering his eyebrows.

"Bye."

"Bye," he said, but she had already ended the call. Had he said something wrong? Maybe she just didn't want to tell him what she got from the store. Maybe it was private, or a female thing. Understanding dawned. "Ohh-hhh," he said. "Maybe I should tread lightly today." He didn't know much about those kinds of things, but he'd heard enough from his married brothers to know that being gentle was the only thing to do.

Colton guided his horse into the barn and dismounted. He took care of his horse and then headed to the house. He didn't see Grace's car out front. What could have taken her this long? He decided the best thing to do was to go get a shower before she arrived. At least he could smell good when he saw her.

A short while later, he walked into the kitchen and found Grace chatting happily with his mom as she stirred something in a mixing bowl.

"Mmm, it smells good in here," he said, walking toward her. He placed a quick kiss on her cheek and tried to gauge her reaction. She gave him a quick smile before turning back to the bowl. "What are we having?" he asked.

"Italian chicken," Mom answered. "Grace is making cheese biscuits to go with it. And she brought a dessert."

"Oh really?"

"Yep," Grace said. "I wanted to show Lydia how her cooking lessons have been paying off."

"They're paying off, even if you didn't learn anything," Lydia said. "I enjoy the company more than the help. But I'm thrilled that you've taken to it so quickly."

"I never knew I liked to cook. But I really do," Grace smiled and her cheeks turned a touch of pink.

Colton was glad to see her brightening a bit. "I think you're a wonderful cook. And if you keep it up, you just might give Mom a run for her money."

That seemed to do the trick, and Grace rewarded him with a grateful look. "I don't know about that, but I'll sure keep trying. You know, I was thinking, maybe I could cook dinner for us one night. You and me, I mean." She pointed at Colton.

He stepped closer to her and put his hand on her arm. "That sounds wonderful. You just name the night and I'll be there."

"We can talk about it later," Grace said, glancing at Lydia, who had turned and appeared to be studying a recipe very intently.

Colton poked her in the ribs, making her jump. "Later it is."

Grace giggled as she turned and reached for a baking sheet. How did she make it look like she had been in this kitchen her whole life? Colton wouldn't know where a baking sheet was if someone paid him to find it. Then again, maybe it was just because she belonged here. Right here, with his family, and in his heart.

Grace slammed the kitchen drawer closed and blew out a breath to curb her frustration. Why had she thought she would be able to cook in her tiny kitchen the same way she did in Lydia's home? She didn't have half the tools Lydia had, and now the oven seemed to have a mind of its own. She looked back at the casserole in disgust. "We can't eat that burned crust," she practically yelled. Maybe if she pulled the top off it wouldn't be so bad. She had just started to test that theory when a knock sounded at the door.

"Come in," she yelled out, not even willing to take her eyes off the food to answer the door.

The door creaked open. "Hey, it's me."

"I assumed it was. Sorry, I'm in the middle of a cooking crisis."

"Oh no, can I help?" Colton's voice was right behind her now.

She tossed the fork onto the counter. "Probably not.

This oven is a piece of garbage. It burned the whole casserole in half the time it was supposed to be baking."

"Oh man. I'm sure it was going to be delicious too," Colton said.

"Now we'll never know."

"It's okay. Why don't we just go to the diner?" he offered.

"Because I was supposed to be making you dinner." Grace could hear her voice rising, even though it wasn't his fault. She told herself to calm down and put a hand to her forehead. "I'm sorry. I'm just mad. I had this great vision of how this was going to go, and this just wasn't it."

"These things happen," Colton said, his voice gentle.

"It wouldn't happen to your mom."

Colton chuckled. "You would be surprised. It doesn't happen often, but that's only because she has years of practice. But I've eaten my fair share of burned food. Cause let me tell you, when she burns it, she does it good."

Grace gave him a look saying she didn't believe him. "Really?"

"Absolutely. Besides, it's probably just the oven. Have you cooked in it much?"

She shook her head. "I don't make a lot of meals just for myself."

"Well, I'm honored that you wanted to make one for me. We can stay here and eat burned dinner. It will probably be a memory we have forever. Or we can go to the diner. Or I've got a better idea. What if we drive to Hillsboro? It will be a little longer, but I don't mind."

Grace felt hopeful at the idea of a dinner date night, but then deflated. "Don't you have to be up early?"

Colton made a face. "Hmm, yeah, actually, I do. We're moving the cattle to the north pasture tomorrow, and we need to get an early start. So maybe we should save that drive for another time. But I would be happy to eat sandwiches and popcorn with you. I just want to spend the evening together."

"I do have popcorn," Grace said. "And turkey and cheese. But that's about it."

"Sounds perfect to me."

"Well, it's not perfect. But we won't starve."

Colton laughed. "That's the spirit."

Grace busied herself looking in the fridge and pulling out plates, then she reached for a bag of popcorn and put it in the microwave. "There. It will be ready in just a couple of minutes." She looked around the kitchen and bit her lip. "I was planning to set the table and eat here, but that seems a little formal for deli meat and popcorn. Do you want to sit in the living room?"

"Sure. Do you want to watch something? We could make it a movie night with a picnic in the living room."

"That does sound nice. The remote is on the couch. The Gibsons ran the cable out here, and they have movie channels. You can pick something out."

Colton made his way to the living room. He had only peeked in from the door other times, but now he looked around the house as he took a seat on the couch. It was small but cozy. Grace hadn't hung any pictures on the wall, and he knew the furniture was here when she rented the house. There weren't any personal touches from her. Was that because she didn't want to spend the money, or because she didn't plan to stay long? She did plan to stay in Shelby Springs, didn't she?

"Here we go." Grace leaned over the couch and handed him the popcorn bowl.

"Thanks," he said. He pointed at the walls. "You haven't decorated much."

Grace sighed as she sat down. She set down a tray of turkey and cheese with pickles and nuts sprinkled around it. "I know. I've never really decorated my own place before. And there aren't a lot of home stores here in town."

"It's not because you are planning to move on?"

"From here? I mean maybe. I'm grateful to the Gibsons, but I don't know if I want to stay here forever."

"Where will you go?"

She shrugged. "I don't know much about real estate in Shelby Springs."

Colton breathed a sigh of relief. "Oh, you mean move out of the Gibsons', not Shelby Springs."

Grace leaned back in surprise. "Of course. Did you think I meant I would move away?"

Colton looked into her eyes. "I hoped not. But it just hit me that you moved here when you knew no one. Maybe you will want to move again to a new place and start over." He shook his head. "I don't know. It's just a thought that came over me, and I wondered if maybe you weren't as settled here as I thought."

Grace reached out and took his hand. "Don't read into it. No, this house isn't decorated, but that doesn't have anything to do with how long I plan to stay here."

Colton smiled. "Okay, good."

"Let's pick a movie."

"No problem." Colton picked up the remote and navigated to the movies. He didn't really care what they watched, as long as Grace was next to him, but he picked out a comedy and hit play. Then he reached for a piece of cheese. He put it in his mouth and closed his eyes. "Mmm, this is the best cheese and turkey dinner I've ever eaten."

Grace laughed. "Me too. I think the company improves it."

"I agree."

They settled back and enjoyed their food from the tray with the popcorn.

"How was work?" Colton asked.

"Fine," Grace said around a bite. "Normal really."

"You said you might not stay in this house, but do you think you'll keep working at the church?"

Grace gave him a strange look. "What else would I do?"

Colton shrugged. "I don't know."

"I won't leave unless there's a good reason."

Colton nodded and turned his attention to the movie. But his mind reeled with questions. If she thought she might get tired of this house, and if she would leave her job for a good reason, would she get tired of him or find a good reason to break up? He told himself he was being ridiculous, but it was still gnawing at him that there was more to her past that she wasn't telling him. Maybe he didn't know her as well as he thought he did.

When the movie ended, Grace cleaned up the dishes from the couch. Colton stood and watched as she made the short distance to the kitchen and returned. He opened his arms and wrapped her in an embrace.

"Do you have to go?" Grace asked.

Colton nodded as he kissed her forehead. "I wish I

didn't, but it's not a good idea for me to be so tired and trying to ride a horse."

Grace sighed. "I know. I want you to be safe."

Colton leaned back to look her in the eyes. "I appreciate that. It means a lot to me that you don't complain about my work. The ranch is part of me. It's an all-consuming part sometimes. I love it, and I always will. But it would kill me if you didn't like it."

"I love the ranch too. It's so different from anything I've ever known. But it's so much better. I might want to complain because it pulls you away from me, but I'm grateful that you work so hard. I know it's important to you."

Colton leaned in and pressed his lips to hers. She responded and wrapped her arms tighter around his waist. He ran his hands up and down her arms, kissing her again and again. He sighed as he pulled back. "I should go."

Grace grinned as she pressed a finger to his lips. "I know. Good night, Colton."

"Good night, Grace."

18

Grace sat at her desk and pressed a finger to her lips. The memory of Colton's kiss had stayed with her.

She sighed thinking about the night before. He was asking a lot of questions, and as much as she enjoyed being with him, it felt pushy. What was he trying to get out of her? Blaine had asked her so many questions when they started dating. She had thought it was nice, at first. She thought he was interested in her and wanted to know her better.

Quickly, those questions became pushier, and her answers were less than satisfying to him. When he asked her a question, she found herself trying to decide what he wanted the answer to be.

She didn't want it to be like that with Colton. She wanted to be open and honest with him, except for her one secret. But all the questions about if she was going to move and if she wanted to keep working for the church felt invasive.

Grace pushed the thoughts aside as she answered a phone call. A church member wanted to use the fellowship hall for a baby shower. Grace confirmed the date and put it on the calendar.

"I'm headed out for a lunch appointment," Pastor Judson said, walking through the office. "I'll be back later."

"See you then," Grace said. That would make for a quiet afternoon. She had brought her lunch and eaten it already. The cheese and popcorn from the night before hadn't held her over too long.

Reaching for her book, Grace settled in, expecting nothing much to happen. Her cell phone rang, and she almost didn't look at it. Not many people had this number, so most of the calls were only recorded messages from telemarketers. But she glanced at the screen and saw that it was a Louisiana number. Her heart pounded at double speed. Maybe her Mom had decided to call her back.

"Hello?" Grace answered.

"Grace."

Her hand flew to her chest and she gasped for breath. No, not him. It wasn't supposed to be him. Her eyes darted back and forth as if she needed to find an exit. She jumped up to run, but reminded herself to take a breath. Squeezing her eyes closed, she told herself he wasn't here. He was only on the phone and he couldn't make her do anything.

"Blaine," she said. "How did you get this number?"

"How do you think?" he said gruffly.

"I guess Mom got my message." But she didn't bother to call her own daughter.

"She was concerned about you and thought it would

be best for me to contact you so we can work this thing out."

Grace felt her blood pressure rising. "There's nothing to work out. I left to get away. I'm not confused, and I'm not changing my mind. I only called my Mom to let her know I was safe."

"Grace, listen. I understand that you wanted some space. It's natural to feel a little nervous before making a lifelong commitment. I'm sorry if I scared you talking about getting engaged. But just tell me exactly where you are and I will come get you. We can put this whole thing behind us and move forward."

"No!" Grace shouted. She moved quickly from behind her desk and moved down the hallway. "No, that's not going to happen."

Colton knew he must look like a high school boy grinning ear to ear as he walked toward the church office. He hadn't planned to come by today, but his mom must have known he needed an excuse when she sent him into town to pick up an order from the feed and seed.

He opened the door, ready to greet Grace. His face fell when he saw she wasn't at her desk. Then he had an idea, and he ran over to her chair and took a seat. She would certainly be surprised when she returned.

Colton jumped when he heard her voice.

"No, that's not going to happen!"

Why was she shouting? Colton jumped up and moved toward the sound of her voice. Was someone with her? No, he didn't hear anyone else, and Grace kept talking.

She must be on the phone. He moved down the hall and realized she was on the other side of the door that led to the sanctuary.

"Blaine, listen to me. I'm not coming back there. You can't make me."

Colton had been ready to burst through the door, but she seemed to be handling this on her own. Suddenly, he heard the voice on the other end. Grace must have put it on speaker phone.

"Look, I've tried to be nice. But you made me look like a fool leaving like that in the middle of the night. And I won't be made to look like a fool. Your parents and I have been telling everyone that you wanted to take a little trip before we set the date for our wedding. I've let you get away with this for long enough. Now, tell me where you are and I will come get you. We will get married, and we will move forward with our life. Your father and I have already made plans for your replacement at work, so you can take care of our home when I become the new Vice President of the company."

"Sounds like you've got it all worked out. But you and my father can do what you want. I'm not coming back, and that's final."

"Grace Rogers, you will not treat me this way. If you won't tell me where you are, I will find you. And I promise you'll regret it."

There was a beep and then silence.

Colton's stomach twisted with a sick feeling. He listened, unable to move in the hallway. It was a long moment before the door swung open, and he stepped back to avoid being hit.

Grace gasped as her hands flew to her face. "Oh, Colton, it's you. You…um, you scared me."

He watched as she tried to compose herself and pasted on a fake smile.

"What are you doing here?"

"I stopped by to see you." Colton kept his expression blank. Would she tell him about the call?

"I'm glad to see you," she said, clearing her throat.

"I was surprised when I didn't find you at your desk."

"Oh right. I just stepped out for a minute."

"Oh? Everything all right?"

A flicker of fear ran across her face, but she waved a hand in the air as she moved back from him and headed down the hallway. "Of course."

Colton couldn't contain it any longer. "I heard you on the phone."

"Oh." Grace dropped into her chair, her face turning white.

"Why weren't you going to tell me?"

She propped her elbows on the desk and dropped her face into her hands. "I don't know. I mean, I wanted to, but maybe this isn't the best time or place." She looked up as tears filled her eyes. "If I told you now I would fall apart, and I didn't want to do that here."

Colton wanted to move to her, to take her in his arms and tell her everything would be all right. But something stopped him. "Why did he call you Grace Rogers? Your last name is Lewis."

Grace broke eye contact. Something like pain and sadness washed across her face as she looked back at him. "No, my last name is Rogers."

Colton put his hand on the wall for support. She had

lied to him. "Who are you? Why did you use a fake last name?"

"Colton, not here. Please."

"This can't wait. If someone comes in, then maybe they need to know the truth too." He moved to the desk and sat down. "I'm ready to hear the truth."

Grace sniffed a few times and wiped at her eyes. "My last name is Rogers. I don't know Grace Lewis. But she had a change of plans and wasn't able to come to Shelby Springs."

Colton put his hand to his chest, wishing he could pull out the knife she was twisting into his heart. "So you stole her identity?"

"I know it sounds awful. But I didn't mean to do it."

"How could you have not meant to?" Colton raised his voice.

"I left my home with one bag and a little bit of cash. I had no idea where I was going. I just had to get away. That day when you found me on the side of the road, I was completely lost. Then you said my name. At first, I was terrified that Blaine had tracked me and you were someone he sent to bring me back. How could you know my name was Grace? Then I realized you thought I was someone else."

"And you didn't tell me any different." Colton crossed his arms, feeling like he needed a barrier between them.

"I wanted to at first. But then I really needed your help. I didn't know how to get my car off the side of the road, and I didn't have a phone to call anyone. You were going to help me, and I thought maybe I could just go along with it for a few hours and then move on. If I disappeared that night, then it wouldn't be a big deal."

Colton hated the thought that she had lied to him, but he also hated the thought that she might have disappeared and he would never have seen her again.

"Then I found myself praying that I could stay here. Everyone welcomed me in. There was a job and a house for me. But every moment I was sure it was all going to come crashing down. That Monday I started work just knowing that it was the last day, but I wanted a little more time in Shelby Springs. Then the real Grace Lewis called and told me her grandmother was sick and she had to go take care of her. She wasn't coming, and that meant I could stay here."

Colton leaned back in the chair. He took a deep breath and blew it out. "But you didn't tell me the truth."

Grace sighed. "I know. And I'm truly sorry for that. But everything else I've ever told you is true. I had to leave because of Blaine. And my name is Grace, only my last name isn't Lewis. I've never lied about anything else."

The silence grew long and uncomfortable.

"I don't know what to say," Colton finally said. "We've spent so much time together, and even if everything else is true, you couldn't tell me?"

"What would have happened if I did? Would you still want to spend time with me? Would I get fired from working at a church? Would the Gibsons kick me out of their guest house? I know that I came here under a false assumption, but I was too afraid to tell you now. I'm too afraid I'll have to leave."

Colton knew she was right about that. He would feel the same way if she told him before as he did right now. That didn't make it okay. He stood. "I have to go."

Grace stood too. "Colton, please, say that you can

forgive me. Say this doesn't mean everything is over." Tears streamed down her cheeks as she pleaded with him.

He looked at her for a long moment, trying to find the words. "I don't know right now. I'm sorry, I have to go."

He turned and walked away from the woman that had consumed his thoughts for some time now. The woman he had thought he was falling in love with.

He let the door slam behind him on his way out.

19

Grace stood in her tiny living room and stared out the window. It had only been a day since she watched Colton walk out of the church office, but it felt like an eternity. She wanted to call him and beg him to talk to her, but it wouldn't do any good. She knew him well enough to know that he was going to make up his own mind.

She should have told him the truth. She knew it. But when was a good time to tell the man you're falling for that you aren't who they thought you were? Every day with him made it a little harder and a little harder, until it became impossible. Anytime she had told him would have turned out exactly how it had yesterday.

But what could she do now? Every time she picked up her phone, she remembered there was no one to call. Colton wasn't ready to talk. She couldn't call Katie; she didn't even know if Colton had told anyone. Her mother obviously didn't care to talk to her. Blaine had sent her several text messages when she didn't answer his calls, but that wasn't who she wanted to talk to.

Pastor Judson must not have talked to Colton. He was concerned when Grace called to say she wouldn't be into work because she wasn't feeling well. She didn't add on to her lie by saying she was sick. There was nothing wrong with her body, but she felt more miserable than she ever had in her life.

At least there was one person she could still talk to.

"God," she prayed, "I messed up, and I know it. I'm not sorry that I stayed here. I think You had a plan for me to be here. But I could have handled it differently. I'm sorry. Now I don't know what to do. Shelby Springs is the best thing that has ever happened to me. No, really, Colton is the best thing. But now I think I might have to leave. If Colton can't forgive me then there is nothing here for me. I love the town and the community and the church. But I can't live here seeing Colton all the time and knowing we can't be together. Not that I can stay anyway. When Pastor Judson finds out, I'll probably lose my job. And when the town knows, they won't feel the same way about me."

Tears rolled down her cheeks. "No, I guess the only thing to do is leave. But I won't go back to Louisiana. I know now for sure that I want something else. Maybe I can find a new small town and start over, with my real name. I can work in a store or something, anything." She sniffed. "Only I'll never fall for someone else."

Colton sulked into the barn. The sun was barely up, and his coffee hadn't taken effect yet. Not that it would help. There was something wrong with him that couldn't be fixed by caffeine. He grabbed his saddle off the wall and groaned as he carried it to his horse. He let the stall door slam behind him and he kicked a bucket out of the way.

Sawyer appeared and leaned over the stall door. "Okay ,Colt, we've let this go on for a week now. What gives?"

"What are you talking about?" Colton pretended not to know.

"You're miserable, and you won't tell anybody why. But we know it has to do with Grace. We haven't seen her since before you got all grumpy. So what happened? Did you run her off?"

Colton huffed. "You don't know the story. Don't make assumptions."

"Okay." Sawyer put his hands on his hips. "Then tell me what happened."

"You won't believe it if I do."

"Try me."

Colton stopped what he was doing and turned to face his brother. "She lied to me."

Sawyer kept his expression even. "About what?"

"About who she is."

"She's not Grace?"

"Well, she is Grace, but not the one who was supposed to come to Shelby Springs to work at the church."

"You're kidding."

"No. Apparently, when I picked her up when her car broke down, I gave her all the information she needed to take her place and dupe us all."

"But her name really is Grace?" Sawyer removed his cowboy hat and scratched his head.

"Yep."

"And did she lie about anything else?"

"She says she didn't, but who knows." Colton shrugged.

Sawyer rubbed his chin. "Hmm. So the only thing she lied about was what you assumed about her?"

"Yeah. I mean the other Grace was coming from Louisiana too, so when I saw the car tag, I just thought it had to be her."

"That makes sense. Do we know why she was really leaving Louisiana?"

Colton nodded. "At least I know what she told me. A bad relationship."

Sawyer stepped back. "So have you let her explain why she lied?"

"Kind of. But it doesn't matter. I can't trust her."

"Hmm," Sawyer said again.

"What?" Colton snapped. "You think I'm wrong?"

"I just think that maybe you should hear her out. Talk with her and see what she says. If she was running from a bad relationship and handed an opportunity to start a new life, then I could see how that would be tempting. I'm not saying it's okay if she lied about everything. But if you said, 'Hey, Grace, welcome to town, here's a job and a place to live,' and she said, 'Thanks, I'll take it,' then I'm just saying maybe it's not as terrible as it sounds to say that she lied and stole someone's identity."

Colton shook his head. "I don't know."

"Listen, just don't make a decision without talking to her. I saw you two together, and there was really something special between you. And I know you were ready to make plans for the future. Don't throw it all away without thinking long and hard about it."

Colton opened his mouth to speak, but Sawyer held up his hand to stop him.

"No, you don't have to explain. If you will promise me that you'll think about it and pray for a few days before you do anything, then I promise whatever you decide I'll stand by you. You're a grown man, and you can make your own decisions. Just give it some time before you do."

Colton turned and went back to his horse. He heard Sawyer go to leave. "Thanks, Sawyer. I promise I will."

Sawyer smiled. "That's all I ask. I'll pray for you too, Colt."

"Thanks, man. I need it."

Grace trudged up the sidewalk to her house after work. She couldn't believe she had managed to go into the office every day that week. Colton hadn't called or reached out, and she hadn't seen him at the office, but he obviously hadn't said anything to anyone else. If Pastor Judson knew, he would have spoken to her about it, at the very least. He probably would tell her to pack her things; they couldn't have someone working at the church under false pretenses.

She pulled the door closed behind her and sighed as she leaned against it. Holding it together at work was one thing, but here at home she could let all her emotions out.

Home.

What a strange thing to call this place that. But it was true. Shelby Springs was the only place she had truly felt welcomed and cared for. This little house on someone else's property was the place she had learned who she really was and who she wanted to be.

But now it was time to go.

She had decided at work that day. If Colton didn't call today, that was it. He wasn't going to. And she couldn't stay here if he wouldn't talk to her.

Since it was Friday, she was done at work, and she could have Saturday to prepare. Not that it would take her long to pack her things. She did have more clothes than she came with, thanks to Katie, and she had a Bible and a Bible study book. But she would take her time putting it all in her car, take one last walk down main street, and eat at the diner. No one would know it, but every conversation would be a good-bye. Then she would leave on Sunday morning while her friends were in church.

Grace dropped onto the couch. Tonight she would watch a movie alone and pretend her world wasn't crashing down around her. But first she had to be honest with Colton about this.

She reached for her phone and typed out a text. The tears rolled as she slowly spelled out each word.

Colton, I'm truly sorry for how I misled you. I didn't mean to, but I did let it go on without correcting you. I should have told you the truth and I'm sorry I didn't. But I know it's too late for that now. I wanted you to know that I'm leaving. I appreciate that you kept my secret this long, but after I'm gone you're free to tell everyone whatever seems best to you. This wasn't your fault. I'll be gone on Sunday morning.

Grace gasped through the sob that escaped as she typed one final line.

I think maybe I loved you, but we'll never know what might have been.

She put her phone in her bedroom and dried her eyes. Picking up the remote, she resolved not to think about it tonight. Something she knew was impossible to do.

COLTON STOOD IN THE FIELD AT HIS PROPERTY. HOW LONG had he thought about building his own house here? Years, it seemed like. Since he was a kid, he couldn't wait to get out of his parents' house and away from the room full of brothers.

Now the property seemed like a lonely place to be.

Would he really build a home without someone to share it with?

He wrapped an arm around his waist to dull the pain. He'd never known a sickness like the feeling of missing Grace. It made him nauseous to think she had been dishonest with him, and it made him miserable to think that he might never see her again.

Colton pulled off his cowboy hat as he sank to the ground and sat. What was he going to do? "God," he called out in the open air. "Why did You bring her here and let me fall for her if this was how it's going to end?"

The silence was deafening.

"What do You want me to do? I don't know if I can trust her. What if everything else she told me is a lie too? What if her name isn't even Grace?"

In that moment, he knew that it was, and that everything else she had told him was true too.

"God, what am I supposed to do?"

Her name echoed again and again in his mind. *Grace. Grace. Grace.*

It wasn't just her name, it was the very thing he

needed. Grace. "God," he spoke more quietly this time. "You've given me more grace than I could ever know. You saved me when I didn't deserve saving and You've given me so many blessings in my life. God, I want to be with her, but I'm still hurt by what she did. Help me to show her grace and forgive her."

Colton squeezed his eyes shut and felt a peace and joy wash over him. He could forgive her. God had brought her here for a reason, and Colton wasn't ready to give that up.

He jumped up from the ground and put his cowboy hat on his head. As he started to walk, his phone buzzed in his pocket. He pulled it out and saw her name on the screen. Could she possibly know what he had just decided?

Dread washed over him as he read the message. Leaving? No, she couldn't. Not when he was ready to move forward. He had to read the message three times to realize she hadn't left yet. "Thank You, God," he whispered. "You brought me to my senses just in time."

He ran for his truck, barely stopping to put his seatbelt on before driving off the ranch. He hoped she hadn't decided to leave sooner. He had to get to her in time.

Colton's heart pounded at double its normal speed as he turned down the road to Grace's house. "God, make her ready to hear what I have to say. I'm ready to forgive her, but I pray she will forgive me too."

As he neared the house, he saw her car in the driveway and breathed a sigh of relief. But he furrowed his eyebrows seeing the second car. Was that one of the Gibsons' kids? Colton didn't recognize it. None of them drove a sports car. As he pulled in, he took a closer look and saw the Louisiana license plate, and his stomach dropped.

The truck was barely in park before he jumped out and rushed to the door. As he neared, he could hear voices shouting inside.

"I'm not going anywhere with you," Grace called out, striking fear in Colton's heart. Was he hurting her?

"Yes, you are. I told you I would find you and bring you back home. You're coming with me whether you like it or not."

That was all Colton needed to hear. He jerked the door open and burst inside.

Grace and Blaine both snapped their heads to look at him.

"That's enough," Colton said.

"Who are you?" Blaine yelled.

"It doesn't matter who I am. What matters is that you're leaving."

"What?" Blaine shouted.

"Let me make it clear." Colton planted his feet and squeezed his hands into fists at his side. "Get out."

"And what if I don't?" Blaine turned to face him.

"I guess you'll have to deal with me. This is Grace's home now, and you will leave her alone. No one is going to make her leave Shelby Springs."

Blaine looked like he was going to step up and punch him. Colton braced himself but felt certain, after years of tussling with his brothers, he could take this guy.

Blaine narrowed his eyes and then dropped his gaze. He turned back to Grace. "Is this what you left for? You want to live in this dump with a guy who smells like cows? Be my guest. I'm done with this."

He bumped into Colton's shoulder as he moved past him to the door, but Colton didn't take his eyes off Grace.

She looked unharmed, but the fear he had seen in her eyes when he came in nearly broke his heart.

"Are you all right?" Colton asked.

She nodded, looking anything but.

He opened his arms, and she closed the distance between them and fell into his embrace. Her body racked with sobs as he held her close. He let her cry without speaking for a few minutes.

Finally, she pushed back and looked him in the face. "Did you mean what you said?"

"Which part?"

"About me not leaving Shelby Springs?"

He nodded slowly. "I meant every word. I don't want you to leave. Shelby Springs is your home, and I know God brought you here for a purpose."

Grace bit her lip. "So you mean you think we can live in the same town? Maybe be friends?"

"Grace, I don't think I could stand being friends with you. I've spent enough time being mad and hurt. And I still don't think it's okay that you weren't honest, but I understand why you did it. I forgive you."

Grace sniffled as her eyes filled with tears again. "Really?"

"Yes, really. We can talk more about it, and we will have to tell my family and Pastor Judson. I don't know how he will feel about it, but whatever happens, we'll walk through it together."

Grace threw her arms around his neck. "I didn't think I could even hope for you to say that," she whispered into his ear.

"We both needed grace in our lives." He chuckled. "And I need you, Grace. You might not have been the Grace we thought was coming, but you are the Grace that I need." He cleared his throat. "And that I love."

Grace leaned back to look at him. "Oh, Colton, I love you too."

He pulled her close to him and pressed his lips to hers. He kissed her with a love he hadn't known possible. They were both breathless when they broke apart. Colton smiled as he stepped back and took her hands in his.

"I don't know what the future holds, but I know who I want to spend it with."

Grace drove down the road as a smile played on her lips. Everything had changed so much in the past forty-eight hours. She had planned to leave Shelby Springs forever on Sunday morning. Now she found herself driving to Whispering Oaks Ranch for dinner with the family. She and Colton had agreed to go together and tell everyone the truth. It might not be an easy dinner, but she felt sure that with Colton next to her, she could make it through anything.

She was only a few miles from the ranch when the car made a funny sound and she felt it wobble. Grace gasped and pulled over to the side of the road. Unbuckling, she stepped out of the car and confirmed her suspicions. "Flat tire," she said out loud to no one.

She climbed back into the driver's seat. "At least this time I have a phone," she said.

Before she could make a call, a pickup truck came into view and she smiled.

Colton pulled over in front of her, stepped down from

the truck, and made his way to her. "What's wrong?" he asked.

Grace stood outside her car and pointed at the tire.

"Are you always this unlucky with cars?" he asked.

She shrugged. "Not usually. But I have no idea when these tires have been changed. We always took it to the dealership."

"Well, you don't have to worry about that anymore. I can take care of it."

"What are you doing here anyway?"

Colton grinned. I decided to drive out and meet you. I planned to stop at the gate, but something told me to just drive until I saw you."

"Good thing you did. I was just about to call you."

"Really?" Colton asked.

"Of course. Who else would I call to save me from the side of the road?"

"Better not be anyone else," Colton said, and he leaned down to kiss her.

"Never anyone but you," Grace said before kissing him again.

"You're exactly who I needed," Colton said.

"Right back at you. We're a perfect match," Grace said.

"I like the sound of that. Will you be my perfect match forever?"

Grace nodded. "Forever."

Hawk Macklin stepped out on the front porch of his family home and sank into the rocking chair.

From here he could usually see clear across the pasture, but today there were a few hundred people blocking his view.

Sawyer walked over carrying his eight-month-old son in his arms. He clapped a hand on Hawk's shoulder. "You don't want to join in the dancing?"

Hawk made a face. "You know that's not really my thing."

Sawyer jerked his chin in the direction of the dance floor that had been set up in the yard. "It looks like Maggie is enjoying it."

The corners of Hawk's mouth lifted into a grin. "Maggie enjoys everything."

"How long have you two been friends now?" Sawyer asked.

Hawk tilted his head. "Mom says we met in first grade,

but I think I mostly picked on her then. I guess we've really been friends since junior high."

"You've known her longer than I've known Katie, and we're married with a kid."

Hawk stood up, knowing where this conversation was going. "Well, you know, marriage isn't for everybody, I guess." He tugged his cowboy hat down on his head. "Come on, let's get started on Colton's truck. It wouldn't be a Macklin wedding without decorating the getaway car."

Sawyer laughed. "You're right about that. You go ahead. I'll wait for Katie to come back and take Dillon off my hands."

Hawk hurried off the porch and found Lawson, Garrett, and Titus waiting off to the side of the crowd. He caught Jenson's eye across the crowd and waved him over, trying to keep Colton from seeing them.

Jenson's jogged over. "Are we decorating the truck?"

"Absolutely," Lawson said.

"You know I'm not missing that. Not after what Colton did to my truck at our wedding."

Garrett laughed. "The feather pillows emptied into the seat was a nice touch."

"You try being the one who has feathers blowing out your windows for a month," Jenson said.

"Don't worry. We've got something perfect planned," Lawson said.

The brothers hurried off to the truck.

Thirty minutes later, they returned to the reception. Hawk couldn't keep the grin off his face. Colton was going to be shocked for sure. He might hate them for it, but that was part of being a Macklin brother.

Hawk made his way to the table and grabbed a slice of cake.

"It was a nice wedding, wasn't it?" Maggie said, stepping to his side.

Hawk nodded and spoke around his bite of cake. "We're getting pretty good at these things around here. This one was different though, not fancy like Katie and Sawyer. It felt right for Colton and Grace."

"Good thing her car broke down where it did that day she arrived."

"That's true. God must have planned that just right. It was rough though, you know. That day when they came and told us that Grace hadn't been honest about who she was."

"I remember when you called to tell me. I was shocked."

"We all were," Hawk said. "But Colton was the first one to forgive her. If he could do that and trust her, we decided we should too."

Maggie nodded. "Oh look, I think they're getting ready to leave."

Hawk nudged her. "Don't you want to go try to catch the bouquet?" He winked.

She pasted on a smile that Hawk recognized as fake. "No, I'm good. Let those teenage girls fight over it."

"In that case, let's get a good view of the brawl."

Maggie smiled then for real.

They watched as Grace threw the bouquet, then Hawk joined the men as Colton threw the garter. Hawk didn't even attempt to reach for it as one of his cousins jumped into the air and caught it.

Then it was time for the big reveal.

Colton and Grace ran over to hug the family and say their goodbye.

Hawk stepped close as Grace hugged his mom. "Thank you for everything."

Lydia Macklin beamed as she looked at her new daughter-in-law. "We're so happy. We love you, and we'll miss you this week."

"Bye, Mama." Colton reached for his own hug.

"My baby boy, all grown up and married," Mom said.

"Don't worry. I won't be far. Although I'm not sad to finally have my own home, and not wake up next to these goobers everyday," Colton said pointing to his brothers.

"You'll miss us soon enough," Garrett said.

Colton laughed. "I doubt it."

"Okay, okay. Enough mushy stuff. Y'all get out of here," Hawk said.

Colton reached for Grace's hand. "Don't mind if we do."

Hawk watched Colton's face as he looked up and saw his truck. His smile faded and he narrowed his eyebrows and gritted his teeth. It faded quickly though. "I guess I deserve this."

"Every bit of it," Jenson said.

Colton laughed. "Come on wife. Welcome to life as a Macklin."

Hawk joined his brothers in laughter as the crowd noticed the truck too.

"How will they get in?" One guest yelled.

"Look at all the bubbles!" A little girl shouted with glee.

Colton and Grace made their way through the mountain of soapy bubbles covering the truck and the ground. Everyone cheered and yelled their congratulations.

As Colton and Grace reached the truck he turned and wrapped his arms around her. The guests cheered as he pulled her close and kissed her.

Colton didn't seem like the youngest brother anymore. Now he was a man with a wife that completed him perfectly.

The Macklin brothers watched as Colton and Grace drove off the ranch into their own happily ever after.

ABOUT THE AUTHOR

Hannah Jo Abbott is not just a writer, but a wife, a mom of four, a homeschool teacher, a daughter, a sister, and a friend. She loves writing stories about life, love, and the grace of God. She finds inspiration and encouragement from reading the stories others share. Hannah lives with her husband and children in Sweet Home Alabama.

For updates on her writing and to receive a FREE novella, sign up for Hannah Jo's newsletters at hannahjoabbott.com/mailinglist.html

facebook.com/hjabooks
instagram.com/hannahjoabbottwriter

Cheeseburger Pie
Ingredients:
- 1 lb lean ground beef
- 1 large onion chopped
- 1/2 teaspoon of salt
- 1 cup shredded cheddar cheese
- 1 cup milk
- 2 eggs
- 3/4 cup flour
- 1 1/2 teaspoon baking powder
- 1/4 teaspoon salt
- 3 tablespoons shortening or butter

Heat oven to 400°F. Grease a 9-inch pie plate.

Whisk the flour, baking powder and 1/4 tsp salt together in a bowl and then cut the shortening in with a pastry knife until the mixture is crumbly. Stir in eggs and milk. Set aside.

In a skillet, brown beef and onion over medium; drain. Stir in 1/2 tsp salt. Spread in pie plate. Sprinkle with cheese.

Pour flour, eggs, and milk mixture into pie plate.

Bake about 25 minutes or until knife inserted in center comes out clean.

Optional toppings: Ketchup, pickles or pickle relish, mustard, mayonnaise, or thousand island dressing.

Billionaire for Christmas Series:

Billionaire Under the Mistletoe

Billionaire at The Christmas Inn